"Wyatt!" She sc... top of her lungs.

Mr. Thomas's steps fal... landed on the grass on her behind with a grunt. Where was her weapon? She had nothing. He was going to kill her now, and there was no way she could fight him off.

But someone did have a gun. *"Wyatt!"*

The glint of a knife flashed in the moonlight. She couldn't see his face, but did that matter? In a minute she would take her last breath, a statistic. A memory.

His hand gripped her hair and pulled her face back to his. "What did you just say?"

"Wyatt," Nina breathed.

"Well. This just got a lot more interesting. I suppose that was the man in your condo? Did you tell him all about me?"

"So what if I did?" she gasped.

"Then he must die, too."

"No—"

Mr. Thomas slammed her head on the ground, and everything went black.

Lisa Phillips is a British-born, tea-drinking, guitar-playing wife and mom of two. She and her husband lead worship together at their local church. Lisa pens high-stakes stories of mayhem and disaster where you can find made-for-each-other love that always ends in happily-ever-after. She understands that faith is a work in progress more exciting than any story she can dream up. Lisa blogs monthly at teamloveontherun.com, and you can find out more about her books at authorlisaphillips.com.

Books by Lisa Phillips

Love Inspired Suspense

Double Agent
Star Witness
Manhunt
Easy Prey
Sudden Recall
Dead End

DEAD END

LISA PHILLIPS

HARLEQUIN® LOVE INSPIRED® SUSPENSE

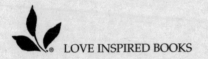

LOVE INSPIRED BOOKS

Recycling programs for this product may not exist in your area.

ISBN-13: 978-0-373-44762-6

Dead End

Therefore, if anyone is in Christ,
he is a new creation; old things have passed away;
behold, all things have become new.
—2 Corinthians 5:17

This year I lost my Granny, Ivy Clayton.
She was 97 years old
when she went to rest in the arms of Jesus.

ONE

Nina Holmes squeezed her hands into fists and resisted the urge to slam them down on the counter. "Ma'am, with all due respect. I'm not leaving until you tell me what I want to know."

Probably not proper decorum for the federal courthouse, but what else was she supposed to do? This woman was her last option. Nina had to get this information.

The name tag read "SONDRA," and it jiggled as she huffed. "Be that as it may, I am only a federal employee. I can't tell you what I don't know."

Nina pushed the creased and worn paper closer to Sondra. "I just need you to contact this person at the other federal courthouse, the one in Baltimore, where these records are kept. They can have the file transferred here. It's so old it's paper, but only an employee of the courthouse can request the file."

Now that Nina was a retired CIA agent, she had zero clout.

Sondra looked at the paper with one penciled eyebrow raised. Nina took a deep breath and launched in. "You see, I'm looking into an old case. It was an FBI investigation into the murder of a congresswoman that took place nearly thirty years ago—my mother. I need this file, Sondra."

It was the one thing she'd never been able to let go of, even in all her years at the CIA running covert missions. Her best friend had been there for her since third grade all the way through their time with the CIA. But now Sienna had gotten married, and they were no longer secret agents for the US government.

Sienna had a new life, and Nina had…nothing but the will to find the truth. That was why she had to look into her mom's death, and maybe even discover the real killer once and for all, so her father—wrongly convicted of the crime—could finally have peace. So that *she* could have peace. Otherwise she was never going to be able to move on with her life.

Sondra fingered the paper.

Nina sighed. "Please, help me."

The woman took the name and phone number of the person Nina had been in contact with in Baltimore—where the murder and trial had taken place. But she didn't pick up the phone. She moved her fingers over the keyboard. The clicking of keys took on a rapid pace, and soon Sondra sat back.

"This person, whoever it is, doesn't show up in my system as working for that particular courthouse." She pointed to the paper. "And that phone number is for the Baltimore public library."

Nina flinched. "What? How is that possible? I called the federal courthouse. I was transferred to that person. He knew about my mother's case. He said he remembered it from the news reports, since the husband killed his congresswoman-wife." Nina swallowed against the bad taste of those words. Her father had been innocent. "He said he would process my request."

"I must be too young to remember it." Sondra's eyes narrowed. "That is what the computer says. I'm sorry I can't help you more." She glanced over Nina's shoulder and raised her voice. "I can help the next in line!"

Nina staggered back. What was going on? She'd thought for sure today would be the day she would finally see the file.

The public library. How could she have been given that number by mistake? None of this made any sense. The process should have been…not easy, but at least possible. She might have worked for the CIA, but it wasn't as though she could just call up one of her old coworkers and ask them for information on a domestic murder that happened years ago.

Nina stumbled down the hall, the injury in her left hand aching beneath the brace she wore to cover the scars. She didn't need the questions, usually innocent enough, but she had no interest in being reminded how she'd gotten the nasty cut. She had more important things to worry about. Her teaching job at the local college would start with the fall semester in a few weeks. Until then the clock was ticking.

It was time to find the killer and put the past to rest once and for all.

She'd walked from the apartment she rented close to the federal courthouse. She lived downtown simply so she didn't burn extra money on a car, insurance payments and gas. The college where she had been hired to teach economics was nearby. A new chapter for her new life.

But so far she was getting nowhere.

Nina blew out a breath and pushed open the heavy

door. The Oregon fall weather was breezy with a pleasant temperature, much different from the biting East Coast air she was used to. Nina hitched her purse higher on her shoulder and tried to push down the frustration while she figured out a new plan of attack. Regroup. That was all she had to do, and the CIA had taught her how. She just needed to come at this from a different angle.

The concrete steps were smooth under her canvas flats. Traffic whizzed past, and two men in bulletproof vests walked a man in an orange jumpsuit up toward her. She stepped aside, too preoccupied to really look at them. They were just doing their jobs. It wasn't their fault she was having a bad day.

But they slowed.

Whether she knew them because Sienna was now married to a marshal or not, Nina didn't want to make small talk. She trotted down the steps onto the sidewalk and turned in the direction of home. Two steps after she had set off, someone yelled her name.

Wyatt? She turned back to tell him she couldn't talk, or wasn't in the mood for it, or some variation of that.

A silver car jumped the curb as it barreled toward her.

Nina didn't have time to scream. She jumped aside and prayed she wouldn't die before she found her mother's real killer, a man who had been having an affair with her mother. A man who called himself Mr. Thomas and who'd told her stories of spies, pirates and fair maidens.

A man no one had ever believed existed when she'd told them *he* killed her mother.

Nina hit the ground and rolled.

Deputy US Marshal Wyatt Ames ensured his partner had hold of the prisoner and sprinted down the steps. The silver car raced away, but he ran to Nina with his gun ready. It was a reflex to draw his weapon, but he wasn't going to shoot at a car fleeing the scene. Too easy to hit an innocent person on a busy downtown street.

Behind him Parker called in the make and model, no plates. Request for EMTs, possible injuries.

"Nina." He crouched beside her and holstered his weapon. "Nina, are you okay?"

She groaned. "No." She sounded mad, which almost made Wyatt smile.

He helped her roll over, which made her groan again. The road rash on her right arm and her temple made him wince.

She eyed him. "That bad, huh?"

He didn't return her smile—there was too much fear in her blue eyes. He did lift her left hand so he could survey the scar from the injury she'd had the day he'd met her. She had a wrist brace on, and he couldn't see the injury on her fingers. Was it under the brace material? That would mean the injury was down by her thumb. Why hadn't he known that?

Wyatt had been there the day they rescued her from the house where she'd been held, months ago now. Caught up in Sienna's amnesia, and the hunt for a flash drive of sensitive information Sienna had hidden before she lost her memory, Nina had been kidnapped in order to draw Sienna out. The man who had held her was dead now, but Nina had been injured.

When they'd found her, Nina's left hand had been bandaged, the wrappings soaked in blood. Yet she'd still been strong enough to push through and help Wyatt's partner—Parker—find Sienna, who was now his wife.

That danger had passed, and Parker and Sienna were finally free to be happy.

Wyatt had been impressed by Nina that day, and it hadn't let up since. Clearly her inner character was as beautiful as she was on the outside, even with the haircut she had gotten recently. He'd never been a fan of short hair on women, but the choppy blond strands made her eyes stand out all the more and he had to admit it was cute.

Wyatt's phone started to ring, but he ignored it. "Don't get up, okay?" Her left hand seemed to have gone through this unscathed, the road rash on her right arm likely from trying to protect the injury beneath the brace. "EMTs will be here in a minute and we'll get you looked at."

Nina sighed and straightened her legs on the sidewalk in front of her. Wasn't she glad help was coming?

"Ames!"

Wyatt turned back to his partner.

Parker motioned over his shoulder with his thumb. "I'm going to check our friend here into his permanent staycation and I'll be back out."

Wyatt nodded and turned back to Nina, still in his crouch. "That was crazy. I can't believe that car jumped the curb and came right at you. Seriously. It was nuts."

Nina's lips curled up, though he could see the pain on her face. "You're babbling."

"Your life just flashed before my eyes."

Nina laughed. He wanted to pull her into his arms and hug her until his heart rate settled down, and she was laughing? "This isn't funny, Nina."

She shook her head. "No, it really isn't. You're right. But to be honest, it's just been one of those days. This is pretty much the perfect end."

"It's not even lunchtime."

"I'm still ready to go home and crawl back into bed. Maybe tomorrow will go better, because today does not seem to be my day."

The ambulance pulled up, a police car parking right behind it. He knew the sergeant who climbed out. Sergeant Zane sauntered over, apparently relaxed, having decided the emergency had passed and Wyatt had whatever this was covered.

The law enforcement community in their town was pretty tight-knit. Zane probably knew Nina through her connection to Sienna and Parker. Being retired CIA agents in this town was enough to make them famous.

Wyatt got up and stepped back as the EMTs started to work on Nina. Zane might think the former CIA agent could handle herself, even in a situation like this, but he hadn't seen the raw fear on her face like Wyatt had. There was a lot of wincing now as the EMT doused her road rash, but she kept it together. All that raw skin had to hurt something fierce, but she held her own. As usual. Did the woman ever break?

Sergeant Zane stopped in front of him. "Parker called in an attempted vehicular homicide. I've got units on the lookout for the car he described, but it seems like it worked out."

Vehicular homicide? Wyatt glanced back at Nina. His head hadn't caught up with his reflexes yet so it took a minute. The car. Nina on the sidewalk. "Why would someone try to kill you?"

It couldn't be easy to have a past full of covert missions—especially when a recent leak made her past career public knowledge. Had someone she'd angered as a CIA agent just tried to retaliate?

Nina looked up, one eyebrow raised. "You're seriously asking me that question?"

Sergeant Zane snorted. When Wyatt glanced at the man, his eyes were on the blue sky. He looked back at Nina. He'd been more concerned about the fact that she was hurt. He hadn't even wondered who was driving the car and why they had done this.

"Who wants you dead?"

Nina cocked her head to the side. "I would write you a list, but..." She lifted her right arm, now being wrapped in a bandage.

Sergeant Zane erupted in chuckles. Wyatt shot him a look that shut him up. Wyatt had been a cop before transferring to the Marshals Service, but couldn't ever remember acting the way Zane did. Now that he was on a fugitive apprehension task force, Wyatt didn't have to suffer the sleepless nights of being a homicide detective. He didn't have to see the tear-filled eyes of loved ones as they faced the gruesome details of death. The long-drawn-out investigations. Awful hours that had taken a toll on every relationship he'd had.

As a homicide detective, he'd had only questions and then had to go out and find the answers. As a marshal he knew the answers—the case was closed—and he only needed to track down the fugitive and dispense justice. When the cell doors shut, his job was done.

The one gray cloud in his life right now was Nina. Or, more specifically, his unwanted feelings for her. Wyatt might have been attracted to her since they met, but Nina wasn't like any other woman. Not exactly a bad thing, but her best friend had just married his partner. She'd have the bug, and if they started dating she'd be thinking about him and "long term."

Not exactly Wyatt's thing, at least when he considered the fact that his track record at relationships wasn't good. It was why he kept everything light. First he had to figure out why he'd never been able to hold on to a relationship. Then he'd open himself up to dating again.

He glanced back at the courthouse, where Parker made his way down the steps toward them. Wyatt looked back at Nina. "What were you doing here?"

Nina opened her mouth to answer, but Parker spoke first. "She was trying to find out who killed her mother."

She shot him a dirty look. "Sienna was *not* supposed to have shared that with you. That was private."

Parker's brows lifted. "You want my wife to keep secrets from me?"

Wyatt glanced between them. They seemed to have this rapport as friends that he didn't have with Nina. And why did that bother him? He moved so the EMT could get by him and head back toward his bus. He heard a low "She's good."

Wyatt nodded to the EMT, then looked back at Nina. "Your mother was killed?" He could see the sadness in her eyes. He'd never seen that undercurrent of grief in her before. Apparently she was as good as he was at keeping things light. "I'm sorry for your loss."

Nina glanced at Parker for a second. "It was a very long time ago. I came here trying to find out what happened. To say I'm getting the runaround is an understatement."

Parker took a step closer to them. "Sienna and I said we'd help."

"Sienna said she'd help. I wasn't even aware you knew." Nina sighed. "And I might have to take you up on your offer since I'm not getting anywhere. I wanted to do it myself, but I might have to face the fact that I'm in over my head with this."

Nina glanced around, still sitting on the sidewalk. Wyatt moved to help her up, but Parker beat him to it. Held out his hand and hauled Nina to her feet while Wyatt just stood there looking inconsiderate.

She gifted Parker a small smile. "Thanks."

"No problem." His eyes were dark, but he had that undercurrent of a happily married man that had for a long time been absent in his partner. "Wyatt is going to take you home, okay? Watch your six."

Finally Parker said something right. Wyatt nodded to his partner, since Nina couldn't see him. She snapped a salute with her good hand. "Yes, sir."

Wyatt shook his head. "Where's your car?"

She turned from Parker as he walked away and said, "I walked here."

"You did?"

She shrugged. "I only live around the corner."

Parker, already ten feet away, spun back. "I'm headed to the office. When you see her home, make sure she eats some lunch."

Nina rolled her eyes.

"My car is this way."

He held out his hand, but she didn't take it. She walked gingerly, and he wished he'd parked closer. She'd hit the sidewalk pretty hard, and she was leaning toward the opposite side. Wyatt put his hand on the small of her back like he was leading her, when the reality was he needed to give her support and comfort even if it was in that small measure.

He'd done the same a million times with witnesses, or women he'd dated, but he'd never felt like this. It was as though a spark of electricity had arced from her to his hand. She probably wasn't even aware of the action, whereas all of his senses had lit up. The lingering rush of adrenaline at watching her almost die wasn't helping. She'd nearly been flattened on the concrete by that car.

She needed support and protection, but from what? The police could track the car, but it was likely stolen. Maybe they would never find out who had been driving. Nina would live the rest of her life under a cloud of impending danger.

Nina's cell phone chimed from inside her purse. She pulled it out and looked at the screen, but he couldn't read the tiny text. What he could read was her reaction.

The flinch.

The quick intake of breath that meant the danger was far from over.

Maybe it was just beginning.

TWO

"Everything okay?"

Nina looked up from her phone. "Yes." She cleared her throat. The text had come from a contact saved in her phone as *Baltimore Public Library*. How was that even possible? Had someone hacked her phone just to send a message?

Next time I won't miss.

She had to talk to Sienna. She'd know what to do. This man whom Nina knew as a friend only, despite the unwanted feelings she had for him, didn't want all of her baggage. No one actually wanted to know what another person's damage was. Every time she'd tried to tell a man she was attracted to about her past, he'd run away in response. She didn't need that all over again. But Sienna was different, best girlfriends were always different.

So Nina kept the text message to herself. Meanwhile Wyatt didn't look like he believed her that it was nothing, but thankfully didn't say anything.

The drive to her building took two minutes, but it was full of awkward silence nonetheless. Nina waved to the doorman and Wyatt did the leading thing again, with his hand on her back. It probably meant nothing. He probably did it with suspects and witnesses all the time. He probably didn't feel the same awareness she did.

They took the elevator to the twenty-second floor. He'd never been to her condo. And why would he have? They'd only hung out at Parker and Sienna's house. What was he going to think? Nina sighed, trying to dispel her ridiculous thoughts. Why did she even care what Wyatt thought? It wasn't like she was looking for a relationship. He was only here because Parker had told him to bring her home.

Nina unlocked her front door. The steady beep of her security system chimed, and she entered the code to silence the alarm. Wyatt was still by her door, eyes wide as he stared at the expanse of her foyer.

"Come in." There were a few boxes she still hadn't unpacked. But the place wasn't unlivable.

Wyatt shook off whatever had stalled him and shut the front door. "Nice place."

"Doesn't have a lot of character, but it'll do for now."

"You're not staying?" He stuck his hands in the front pockets of his jeans, which pulled his shirt taut over his arm muscles.

Nina looked away. "I thought about buying a house, but who wants to mow a yard? If I want to have a country experience I'll go to Sienna and Parker's house in the sticks."

Wyatt eyed her. "Some people like that kind of thing." He glanced around. "So this is home?"

Home. There was a concept Nina didn't know all that much about, unless he was talking about her friendship with Sienna. They'd been each other's family for years. Instead of answering, Nina went to the kitchen and pressed the button on the side of her coffeepot, where it heated water. After the morning she'd had, she needed hot chocolate, stat. Maybe even marshmallows.

"Do you want coffee?"

He was looking at her like she was a puzzle he hadn't realized was five thousand pieces and not six simple ones easily slotted together. "Sure. Parker said something about lunch." He sauntered to her fridge and pulled it open. "How about eggs?"

"Sure."

She made the drinks while he pulled ingredients from the fridge. "Where's the sausage?" His eyes narrowed. "The fancy cheese I get, but you eat meat, right?"

Nina smiled. "Bottom drawer."

Wyatt muttered "thank you" and stuck his head back in the fridge. Nina chuckled as she circled the center island, where the burners were. Her side was a counter on which he set a chopping board, an onion and a handful of mushrooms, then slid over a knife.

"You're on chopping duty."

Nina smiled. "I'll make you proud."

She got to work cutting veggies as best she could with her right hand while Wyatt's strong hands cracked each egg with ease—though who would eat all of this food was anyone's guess. But even with the easiness of their friendship, the weight of the day washed back like the incoming tide. It always did, and Nina wasn't sure she'd know what to do if one day she no longer had to worry about it.

"Tell me what all this is about."

The knife slipped across her finger, and Nina cried out. Wyatt rushed around the island and pulled her to the sink. He ran the cold water gently over her right hand and held her finger there. The liquid washed away the drops of blood and helped numb the pain. Too bad something so simple didn't work on everything.

He ran his thumb over the tiny cut. "It doesn't look too bad, but you should put a bandage on it."

Nina got one from the end cupboard and sat so he'd know she didn't need his help. She finished the rest of the chopping without speaking, and then pushed the cutting board to his side of the island. He looked up from stirring, evidently content to wait for her to be ready to answer his request.

"My mother was killed, you know that. Parker said it. Her name was Congresswoman Clarissa Holmes." Nina sucked in a breath. "When I was five years old my parents separated for a while. My mother began having an affair with another man."

Nina clenched her fingers together in her lap, but it hurt so she let go. "I would see him when the nanny brought me home from the park. His name was Mr. Thomas, and he was very handsome. He would have tea with my mother and me every day, and he would tell me stories about pirates, and fair maidens, about spies and bad guys. I think he was one of them. A spy, I mean.

"Maybe he's part of the reason I said yes when the CIA wanted to recruit Sienna and me. I looked for him in their databases as much as I could, but never found a single trace of anyone with the first or last name of Thomas who looked like him. Maybe I was wrong about him being a real spy, but that's what I thought for a long time. Anyway, one day—I was six and a half, I think—we came home from the park and the front door was open."

Wyatt slid the eggs into two bowls and came over. He sat on the stool beside her, but didn't say anything.

"She was in the bedroom. There was blood everywhere. The nanny started screaming, so I ran to the study and called 911 from the phone. She fled out the front door and left me there. The police found me, on the stairs. Alone in the house with my dead mother."

"And the police thought your father did it?"

"It was his letter opener. He'd left it when he moved out, but he hadn't been there in months. I was sent to live with my grandparents, and they shipped me off to boarding school. I don't think they were too interested in another child, especially one who had gone through a trauma.

"I went to see my father after I turned eighteen. He said it wasn't him, and he wasn't lying. It never seemed right to me that he had just shown up that day and killed her. But the police never believed me about Mr. Thomas." Nina blew out a breath. "I've been thinking it through ever since."

Wyatt nodded.

"When I told the police about Mr. Thomas they thought I had invented him to cover for my father. They never found the nanny—she just disappeared. No one else knew anything about the man who'd been spending all that time with my mother. They thought he didn't exist because she hadn't told anyone—not her friends, or employees—about him. They even tried to get this counselor to say I was making the whole thing up, like I was hysterical or delusional or something. Like I'd made up the idea of another suspect just so they wouldn't send my father to jail."

Nina squeezed her eyes shut. "I was the kid in school

whose father killed her mother and who made up a story. The crazy child no one wanted their kid to hang around with because my delusion might get them killed, too."

"Except Sienna."

"She was as alone as I was, and she didn't care what anyone else thought."

Nina had worked for years with her best friend, Sienna. Playing bad guys off against each other, rehashing missions that had gone bad. They had been friends since that first day of third grade at boarding school, and they'd been inseparable ever since.

Except that Sienna had married Parker a couple of months back. Nina didn't begrudge the happiness Sienna had found with the marshal. Sienna certainly deserved it after she was attacked on a mission and got amnesia. Nina had tried to help her remember where she'd hidden the sensitive information, which had presented a significant breach of national security. Sienna and her husband had cleared all that up, though, and fallen in love in the process.

But Nina couldn't help feeling like maybe she'd been left behind.

Wyatt returned her smile. "And…now you're trying to find this Mr. Thomas guy? To prove that your father is innocent and get him out of prison?"

"My father is dead."

Wyatt swallowed against the lump in his throat. "I see."

An innocent man had died in prison? There wasn't much that Nina would achieve by unearthing something everyone else involved probably considered over and done with. He didn't like it, but things were what they were. Still, the look on her face pricked his heart.

"I could…make some calls." He took a breath. "Find the original investigating FBI agent, see if I can maybe get you a copy of the file."

If she saw the evidence against her father for herself then she would know why he'd been put away. Maybe after that she could be convinced she didn't need to continue on this fruitless search. Wyatt wasn't discounting her memories, but she had been a child. Whether her mother had been having an affair or not, her father had been convicted for a reason. The evidence had to have been conclusive, or there would never have been a guilty verdict.

He believed in the justice system, despite its flaws. Wyatt believed if the evidence hadn't been there, then the wrong person would not have been sent to prison.

"You would do that?" Nina's look was full of hope, of wonder, that he might be able to help her. "Could you get the file?"

Wyatt nodded. "It's worth a try." He had a cousin who was an FBI agent that he could ask. If only to put to rest her questions, and this search she was on, to find a truth that was likely anything but. It'd be worth a call to help her do what he'd had to.

Move on.

Have you, really?

"Thank you." She jumped up and put her arms around him.

Wyatt was taken aback for a moment, but remembered himself fast enough that he could return the hug before she got embarrassed over what she'd done. When was the last time someone had hugged him to say thank you? He wasn't sure he could remember.

When they'd eaten, he set the dirty dishes in the sink and wiped his hands on a towel. "I should head back to the office, but I'll make some calls this afternoon."

Nina looked up at him from her perch on the stool. Her big blue eyes were full of sadness, and possibilities. It was enough to convince him she was onto something, despite the evidence to the contrary. Her need to prove that things had been the way she remembered them was strong, he got that. He understood why someone would want to preserve their memory of what had been—to prove what she knew to be true. But she was talking about events that happened when she was a young child, and since then she could easily have distorted things in her head.

Children were notoriously bad witnesses when any time had passed. Often they only wanted to tell adults what they wanted to hear—or what they themselves wanted to believe had happened. Was that the case here?

"Thank you, Wyatt."

He nodded. The wall he could see in the living room caught his eye, so he trailed toward it. Nina jumped up and intercepted him. "Didn't you just say you had to get back to work?"

Wyatt looked at her.

"There's nothing interesting in there."

Except that he thought there were printed pages or even newspaper articles tacked to the portion of the wall he could see. Why didn't she want him to go in there and look? Nina wasn't exactly hiding what she was doing. Parker and Sienna obviously knew about her looking into her mother's murder, and she'd told him without too many qualms.

"If you say so." But he didn't believe her.

If she'd tacked pictures and news releases on the wall in her living room, this was clearly worse than he'd thought. It had consumed her daytime hours, which meant it also consumed her nights, too. Parker seemed to think she had to be reminded to eat. The signs were all there.

Nina was obsessed.

He understood why well enough. He'd been there himself even, but he knew what the end would be. If Nina kept going, either she would destroy herself trying to find the answers, or she would reach the end and find not even an ounce of the satisfaction she'd been looking for. She was going to wind up empty and exhausted with no answers.

"I guess I'll be going then." He stepped back. "Have a nice rest of your day."

Wyatt walked to the door. That hadn't been a great thing to say. Nina didn't need the brush-off. What she needed was someone who could be compassionate to her situation—and that just wasn't Wyatt. Sympathy, yes. But he didn't know how much more he could give her when it would probably be unhelpful.

He turned back to her. "Be careful, and let me know if you need anything."

But it couldn't be denied she also needed someone who was going to tell her the truth—her father likely *was* her mother's murderer. That the man she thought had done it didn't have any reason to have killed her mom, not if they were in a relationship. She'd said herself that they had been happy, her mother and this "Mr. Thomas."

"Goodbye, Wyatt." Her voice was small, damaged. She didn't sound anything like the self-assured former CIA agent he'd come to know.

A woman who had nearly died today.

Wyatt pulled out his phone before he hit the elevator. It rang twice and Sergeant Zane answered. "Hey, I need a favor."

He felt better after he'd ordered regular drive-bys of her building to check for suspicious activity that could be another attack. There wasn't much else he could do aside from 24-7 protection, but Wyatt still drove away racking his brain for other things that might help. Whoever had tried to kill her with that car would most likely try again.

And Wyatt was going to be there when he did.

THREE

The *click* of the front door echoed through the foyer. Nina's socks whispered on the floor as she trailed to the living room. The walls were covered with sketches she'd done from memory after she'd learned how to properly execute a suspect drawing, but weren't useful at all in identifying Mr. Thomas. Articles she'd printed from archived newspapers detailed her mother's murder all the way through the investigation to the sentencing…and then finally her father's death in prison.

It was a play-by-play of the worst days of Nina's life.

She kept them up as a reminder and as a memorial. She couldn't let anyone in, not without knowing their true motives. Nor was she prepared to open herself up— except to people like Sienna who convinced her otherwise. Not when there were people in the world who would slit a woman's throat even knowing the woman's child was on her way home.

Nina turned a full circle to look at the sum of her life now. Her search for the truth would enable her to move on, and the teaching job would begin the next chapter of her life. She just had to find Mr. Thomas before fall semester started.

The floor creaked.

She spun again, half expecting Wyatt to have come back for some forgotten thing. It wasn't him.

Mr. Thomas stepped into the room.

He wore a suit, much the same as the last time she had seen him, years before. His hair was gray but still stylish, and his tan was highlighted by the pale lines on the sides of his face where he'd been wearing sunglasses.

"Hello, Nina."

Nina's feet were frozen to the floor, her muscles solid. "It's you," she said. The landline phone was three feet to her right on the end table beside the couch. Could she get there? What did he want?

Mr. Thomas's cheekbones were high, his lips pursed as he surveyed her. For an old man, he was remarkably handsome. Probably in his seventies, at least, but he could easily pass for someone younger. Nina could almost see how a woman could fall for his charm—not knowing he was a murderer. A murderer who'd come to kill her.

"Why are you here?" The question left her lips before she realized she said it. Did she want to engage him or just run?

His eyes flickered. "You tell me, Little Mouse."

Lunch turned over in Nina's stomach. He'd called her that, and she'd forgotten until now. *Little Mouse.* "Why did you kill her?" She wanted to know. She needed to know why he had murdered her mother. Though no reason on earth could justify what he'd done, she still demanded the reason. "Why?"

She didn't see a gun, but it could be behind his back. He could be carrying all manner of weapons—just like she had hidden around her condo. Now she just had to make it to the closest one so she could force him to leave…after she got him to admit what he'd done.

It was a shame she couldn't record his confession.

"I'll take the first question." The words rolled from his mouth as sweetly as a frozen treat.

She repeated it. "Why are you here?"

"Curiosity, I must admit. That is the biggest reason." He halfway grinned. "That my Little Mouse has come back after all these years, scurrying around and trying to dig up information best left buried. For everyone's sakes."

"Because you killed my mother."

"And you won't let it rest."

"Why should I?" Nina asked. "Why ever would I let you get away with it when I can get the evidence—"

"There is none to be found."

"I'll figure something out."

"A confession?" He sneered. "Unlikely."

"Shame I don't have a recording device." She shot him a look in return. "But now I know you're threatened by me digging into the past. Otherwise you wouldn't be here. And you certainly wouldn't have tried to run me over earlier."

"A simple scare tactic. I had considered it beneath me, but I can't deny there was a certain…rush. It turned out to be quite a pleasant excursion."

"How nice for you." She accented the last word and lifted her right arm to show him the road rash she'd acquired to keep from hurting her left thumb any more than it already was. There was no need to let him know she'd been scared out of her wits. "All to warn me off getting my mother's file?"

"No one will benefit from the past being resurrected,

Little Mouse. Some things just need to be laid to rest and left undisturbed."

"Not when my father was wrongly convicted. Not when he died in prison before he ever got the chance to be exonerated. I've spent years trying to find you, trying to bury what happened. But I can't escape it. I can't seem to escape you." Nina sucked in a breath. "And now I suppose you're here to kill me, too?"

She needed to know either way. The not knowing was making her antsy, and then she would say something to attempt to end this and wind up making it worse. Nina prayed she hadn't just done that anyway.

"Perhaps."

Nina rushed to the phone, snapped it up and pressed the button. He hadn't moved or made any attempt to come after her. When she listened and heard no dial tone, he laughed. "Nice try."

Nina threw the phone handset and the base at him. The cord snapped taut and it landed on the couch. The closest weapon was in the kitchen, as was her cell. There was pepper spray in the hutch and a baton under the couch, but one was too far and the other she had to crouch low for.

Nina looked around for what else she could throw at him. The lamp, maybe?

He drew something long and thin from his pocket. Did she even want to know what was in that needle? Nina reached for something to say that would divert his attention. "So you've been keeping tabs on the case all this time?"

"My work is to be appreciated. Of course I stay connected."

"And you tried to run me over because I was asking

about my mother?" They'd already been over this point, but misdirection involved confusion. She needed to make him wonder if she was the one misinterpreting their conversation, or if he was.

"Nice dive, by the way."

"The truth has to come out."

Mr. Thomas frowned. "Not the right choice." His face had reddened, and the vein on his neck puckered. "I'm afraid I can't let that happen, Little Mouse. That's why you're coming with me."

"You're the one barking up the wrong tree, Thomas."

"That's *Mister* Thomas," he hissed.

Nina stood straighter. At the first chance, she had to run for her phone. She couldn't let him best her, couldn't let him take her where he'd be able to kill her and bury her. Not when no one would ever know what had happened. She would be the victim. Yet another mysterious death, with only herself to blame.

He came forward then. "Come quietly, Little Mouse. It will be better for both of us."

She shook her head. "No way."

He lunged. Nina ducked and kicked out with her leg. The close proximity of the couch meant she didn't get as much momentum as she wanted, but she slammed his knee as hard as she was able.

Thomas grunted. He swung out with the needle and she slammed her forearm into his. They grasped each other's free hands and grappled. Strength for strength matched in a battle for her life.

Nina gritted her teeth and struggled. He was older, but muscled. She had training.

Eyes locked with his, she kicked out again.

As though expecting it, he countered the move. Pain

burst in her shin and Nina's grip loosened. She pushed back against his hands hard enough to shove him two steps back, then turned and ran the couple of steps to the end table, and the lamp.

She whipped it around at the same moment she felt a sting in the back of her shoulder. Nina rotated and slammed him on the side of the head with the lamp. The needle end broke off, still stuck in her shoulder.

Thomas cried out.

Nina ran for the kitchen. She cleared the doorway far enough ahead of him to pick up her cell phone. Her fingers were slick, but she'd preprogrammed a quick-dial setting while Wyatt was cooking lunch.

"Nina?"

A hand grabbed her hair and yanked.

Nina dropped the phone and screamed as she was dragged backward. The phone cracked on the tile floor as he pulled her across the threshold into the hall.

Wyatt pushed open the door of Nina's building to the sound of sirens from approaching police cars. He hit the button for the elevator and tapped his foot as the car ascended to the twenty-second floor. "I'm sure she's okay." He muttered the words into the empty car, not because he was actually convinced. More like trying to fool himself into believing it.

Wyatt just wanted to get up there. He'd called Nina back after she screamed, and then he'd called Parker. Neither he nor his partner had gotten through on either her landline or her cell phone during the ten minutes since her call, until now.

He drew his weapon as the elevator slid open to reveal the building's security guard outside the door to Nina's condo. "She isn't answering, but there's thumping. Like I said on the phone, sounds like someone is in there with her," the guard reported.

Wyatt nodded. "You did good, waiting for me."

The couple of minutes had probably felt like a lifetime. Still, Wyatt didn't want an old security guard getting hurt. Wyatt turned away, lifted his foot, and kicked the door open. He swung around, gun up, and started a room-by-room search.

"Nina?"

Kitchen was clear. Her phone was broken on the floor, a path through the debris like something had been swept through it. The hall looked exactly the same as when he'd left not long ago.

A dark figure crossed the hall at a dead run.

Wyatt raced after him into the bedroom. He'd clearly spooked the man, but was it in time to save Nina? The balcony door was open. Air blew back the long curtain with the night breeze. The man glanced over his shoulder, half out of the window.

"US Marshals."

The man just stared. Long enough for Wyatt to get a good look at his face. Silver hair. Regal nose. The man shoved at the screen and jumped out. Wyatt raced to the window, where he rappelled from a rope attached to the balcony down to the ground floor. Who was this guy?

He called in what had happened to the police and requested roadblocks and a sweep starting where he landed. "Nina?"

"In here," Sienna yelled.

He ran to the living room, where nearly the whole team had arrived. "You're here."

Parker nodded, on his phone.

A socked foot was visible at the far end of the couch, and a broken lamp lay discarded on the floor. Sienna huddled over Nina. Wyatt rounded the couch, stowed his weapon and crouched. Nina was facedown on the floor. New raw red scratches covered her right hand and forearm. He brushed back hair from the side of her face and winced.

"Nina. Can you hear me? Nina?"

She didn't move.

Sienna grabbed his hand. "Parker's calling an ambulance."

Nina's head felt like an elephant had sat on it. She blinked against the fluorescent lights of the room and looked around. Not her bed. Not her clothes, a hospital gown.

Beside her, on a chair, Wyatt Ames sat with his head in his hands.

"Hey," she managed to say.

"You're awake." He shot up from the chair and perched on the side of her bed. "How are you feeling?"

Nina tried to swallow against the arid desert in her mouth. Wyatt reached for a cup and held the straw to her. Nina pushed up on the bed. "I can sit up."

"Okay, but take it easy."

She took a drink. There was a knock on the door, and two cops entered. Wyatt nodded to them, and then asked, "Want to tell me what happened?"

Nina pushed back the hair that hung over her eyes, the ends tickling her cheek. "Sure."

One of the officers pulled out a little notepad and a pencil. How could they arrest Mr. Thomas when she—or they—didn't even know the man's whole name?

"But I don't know how much good it's going to do."

Wyatt replaced the cup on the table. "Let us worry about that. I gave a statement myself. I saw his face, and I'm going to head to the office after this to look at mug shots and see if I can identify him."

Nina nodded. It hurt enough to breathe that she wondered if Thomas might have cracked a rib or two. "He was in my condo after you left. He was mad because I wasn't prepared to go with him. He was going to drug me, but the needle end broke off. I called you and it connected, and I yelled, and it was like he…snapped."

"He?"

Nina shut her eyes. She could see his enraged face as he stood over her. Fine, if Wyatt needed her to identify the man aloud, she would do it. Nina steeled herself and opened her eyes. "It was Mr. Thomas."

She caught Wyatt's surprise before he could cover it. "The man in your condo was the man you believe killed your mother?"

He thought it was someone else? "I *know* he killed her. He as much as admitted it."

Wyatt swallowed what he'd been about to say. Had he thought the suited, silver-haired man in her apartment was some kind of thug?

Nina sighed. "I know you don't believe me. I know you think that I just want to believe it wasn't my father and that I'm making up a story."

Wyatt started to shake his head. "That's not—"

"I'm not asking you to believe something you don't know, Wyatt. You weren't there that day, but I *was*. My father didn't do it. It *had* to have been Mr. Thomas. There's no other explanation."

She sucked in a breath to control the riot of emotions.

Tired and beat-up, she probably wasn't in any frame of mind to do this. But if Mr. Thomas thought she was going to leave things alone now, he was delirious. There was no way Nina would let this lie. Not after he'd attacked her.

She gritted her teeth. "He found out I've been asking questions about my mother's death, and he came after me because of it. That means he's guilty."

She turned to the officers and gave them her mother's name. The date. If she'd had the file already she'd have given them the FBI's case number.

Nina turned to Wyatt. "Did you call the FBI and ask them about the file?"

He shook his head. "Not yet, but I will."

It hadn't been long since he'd made lunch in her kitchen. She hoped he really would do that. She had a serious problem with anyone who said they were going to do something and then didn't, and she had ever since her life had been consumed with warring parents who made outlandish promises to her just to one-up each other. They had never found it necessary to keep their promises. Then one day both of them were gone.

Wyatt frowned. "We should let you rest. Not that they think any of the tranquilizer in that needle got into you. It's being tested for fingerprints. But still…"

Nina lay back in bed. Her shoulder was sore where the needle had broken off inside her. But fingerprints? She didn't think he'd been that careless. Had he been wearing gloves? "It was Mr. Thomas who tried to run me over this morning. It was him who pretended to be a clerk at the federal courthouse in Baltimore to keep me from getting the file."

What else was she forgetting to tell him?

Wyatt shook his head. "I just don't want you to worry

yourself. You should worry about resting until you're healed."

Nina shot him a look. Wyatt opened his mouth to argue with her, but the door swung open.

"She's awake?" Sienna rushed in, Parker right behind her. She virtually shoved Wyatt out of the way and hopped up on the bed.

The two officers slipped out before the door shut. Wyatt got up, and he and Parker huddled in the corner to converse quietly about who knew what. Probably the imaginary man who had killed her mother and how she could have dreamed up him being in her condo—and attacking her.

Okay, so she was making assumptions. He had said that he saw Mr. Thomas himself. Maybe Wyatt was starting to believe her.

Nina found herself enveloped in a hug. She blinked back tears, and her friend leaned back with Nina still in her embrace. Sienna tipped her head to one side. "He found you, and now he's trying to kill you?"

"Looks that way."

"So now we have to find him and catch him first?"

"You're married. Why would you want to be traipsing around after someone who no one thinks exists when you could be at home doing…I don't know what. Dusting?"

Sienna blinked. "You think I dust?"

"Okay, maybe not." Her best friend hired a cleaner. Sienna had always hated cleaning toilets, and basically every other part of housekeeping except baking. "But seriously…" Nina shifted her eyes toward Parker, and then back at her friend.

"Parker will help. He does that." Sienna smiled.

For years it had been the two of them. Did Nina have

to actually like the fact that Parker was around all the time now? Sienna didn't have to rub her face in it.

"You're not smiling. You have grumpy face." Sienna paused. "Does it hurt that bad?"

Nina shrugged.

"While you were on the floor of your condo, Wyatt chased Mr. Thomas out your bedroom window. I heard him giving the description to the cops. He saw him."

Nina slumped back on the bed. Wyatt, chasing a man like Mr. Thomas from her place. Then he sat there like it was no big deal to her, and just asked questions. As though she was some witness he had to get information out of. "I'm tired and sore."

"Maybe so, but you're also mad. I'll make some calls and we'll find out who this Mr. Thomas guy was. Is." Sienna's eyes were narrow. "Then he'll know why it's a bad idea to try and do in my best friend."

Nina rolled her eyes, though she didn't doubt her friend's skills. She had been keeping Sienna updated on her lack of progress, but that didn't mean her friend was going to be involved in clearing Nina's father. If Mr. Thomas was going to show up and do things like this, Nina wasn't going to let the outcome ripple outward and hit people she cared about. Innocent people.

"Just let me know what you find," Nina said. "I'll figure out what to do about it."

Sienna didn't look impressed.

"She's right." Parker set his hand on her shoulder. "And yes, Nina, we'll pass you and Wyatt whatever we find out."

Wyatt? Why did Parker think his partner was involved in her business? Lunch had been Parker's idea, and she might have called him, but that didn't mean there was anything between them.

"That's our cue to go." Parker escorted Sienna to the door, but not before she gave Nina one last light squeeze.

Wyatt stepped over to her, but she didn't look up.

"What's with the face?"

Nina ignored Wyatt's question and hit the button for assistance. As soon as a nurse or doctor came in she'd find out how long she had to stay here. Then she could continue her search. Because now that she knew for sure Mr. Thomas had killed her mother, there was nothing to stop Nina from figuring out who he really was.

But first she had to deal with Wyatt. "I actually have a question."

Wyatt sat on the end of the bed. "Shoot."

"Why are you still here?" Did he feel guilty he hadn't been there when Mr. Thomas came in, or that he hadn't checked out her condo before he left? That wasn't something he needed to take upon himself. She was a trained former CIA agent. She didn't want him to stick around if that was the reason.

"A bad thing happened to you today." His face was neutral, unreadable. "I rode in the ambulance with you, and I wanted to see that you were okay."

"You did."

Doubt flashed across his face. "Do you want me to leave?"

Usually he acted like he couldn't wait to leave her presence. Not today after lunch, but previously when they'd hung out as a group.

Nina sighed. She couldn't deny it was nice to not be alone. Plus she kind of thought Wyatt felt guilty for the fact that Mr. Thomas had gotten away.

"Maybe you could…stay until the doctor comes."

"I could do that." His eyes flashed, but he sobered fast. "I'm sorry I wasn't there when Mr. Thomas came in."

"He wouldn't have come if you had been, and you couldn't have stayed forever. You didn't know."

"But you did, and I didn't believe you. And now a killer is loose." He pulled a phone from his back pocket. Her phone. He swiped the screen and then held it up.

The text message. That was the thing she'd forgotten to tell him, the text from Mr. Thomas now obscured by the shattered glass of her phone's screen and the edges of the clear tape he'd covered it with.

"You want to tell me why you didn't mention earlier that this killer threatened you?"

FOUR

Wyatt set his mug on the coffee table and sat, still in his pajamas. Sleep had been a pipe dream, especially after Nina shut down and refused to tell him anything more when he'd confronted her over the text. She hadn't shared it with him. She hadn't trusted him. If she'd told him about it Wyatt would never have left her alone at her condo.

Nina had been admitted to the hospital overnight, and when the doctor mentioned it she'd looked relieved. It made no sense to him why anyone would choose the hospital over home, but she had to be monitored for a possible concussion. So here he was, just before six in the morning, on his couch.

He held the phone to his ear and listened to it ring. He needed a sounding board, and who better than his cousin, the FBI agent?

Geoff's voice was chipper, as always. "Up early, aren't you, coz?"

Wyatt smiled and relaxed back into the corduroy cushions. "Whereas you probably didn't even go home last night." His cousin lived on the East Coast where the FBI was headquartered, and he refused to lose. Ever.

"Actually I went to the gym at four after the debriefing wrapped up, and then I went home to take a shower and came back to work. For the record."

Wyatt snorted. "Overachiever." Neither of them had slept, then. Wyatt probably looked a whole lot rougher. He certainly felt it.

"So what's up with my favorite Oregon cousin this morning?"

"Nothing your very-special-agent, East Coast self can't help me with. So get your Fed fingers moving across that keyboard and find me whatever you can on the murder of Congresswoman Clarissa Holmes."

A choking sound erupted on Geoff's end of the phone. "Congresswoman who?"

"It happened thirty years ago."

"Thank goodness. I thought you'd stumbled on something big. I would have owed you." Geoff made a shuddering noise.

"I didn't say I hadn't," Wyatt said. "Now type."

"Congresswoman Clarissa Holmes?"

Wyatt rattled off the date of the murder, which he'd gleaned from the crime lab's sweep of Nina's apartment and the array of documentation she had detailing her mother's life—and her death.

Geoff made a negative buzzer noise. "Nada. Next question."

"Nothing?"

"Crime predates electronic files. When it was entered into the official record, the file would have been incinerated and only the evidence kept. What I have onscreen are the bare bones of a file that is curiously missing pertinent details—not sure why it wasn't all filled out correctly. I have only key elements that would confirm it's the right case, and a note about a fire at the evidence storage facility. That's all."

"You're kidding me."

"So basically I got nothin' but an address and a date."

If the evidence had been destroyed and the file altered, that couldn't be good. Clarissa Holmes's murder had to have been a big deal. Could it be a coincidence that Nina's father was dead and the evidence had been conveniently burned to a cinder? Wyatt didn't believe it. Not considering the fact that Mr. Thomas was alive and well, and very aware Nina was looking into this. Could he have set the fire that destroyed the evidence?

"Sorry, Wyatt." Geoff paused for a minute. "You know, an internet search says the husband did it."

"He died in prison." Wyatt explained about Nina, his connection to her and how "Mr. Thomas" had shown up at her house the day before. "She needs help."

"That much is clear."

Wyatt didn't like that tone. "Hey—"

"No, I know you, Wyatt. You get suckered in by a pretty face and a sob story and you're running errands for this woman. Next thing you know, you'll be asking me to reopen the...wait a second."

Wyatt waited for the rest, but it never came. "What?"

"The case isn't closed."

Wyatt shook his head to his empty living room. "You just said the husband was convicted."

"Hang on." Geoff was quiet for a couple of minutes.

Wyatt sipped his coffee and tried to figure out what on earth was going on. What if Nina was telling the truth? He'd ruled out her having some kind of delusional episode brought on by the stress of being kidnapped months ago and almost having her thumb cut off. He'd seen the man in her bedroom, after all. And he'd read the text message she hadn't wanted to explain to him. Wyatt had drawn his own conclusions on that one.

He hadn't really thought there was more to her mother's murder than what he assumed the Feds had discovered. There was no way they'd have garnered a conviction without it. A federal case couldn't be based on a confession alone—they had to have had evidence.

He didn't know what to think about "Mr. Thomas." At the moment none of this really made sense to him, but one thing was clear. Nina needed help. And if Wyatt could help her, then he should do it. He owed as much to Parker. He'd been a good friend to Wyatt for years, and Sienna had made his life better.

Wyatt couldn't deny that their faith had a lot to do with it as well. But the two of them had been through so much, and if Wyatt could make their happy times easier by helping their friend, then he was going to do everything he could to make that happen.

"Okay, I got something. But it makes no sense."

Wyatt said, "What is it?"

"The file…it isn't really open, but it's not closed either."

"You're right. That makes no sense."

Geoff huffed. "It looks like it's been flagged. There's an active investigation into a string of murders. They have to be similar somehow, but I'd have to look into each one to figure it out. Clarissa Holmes's murder is possibly connected."

"Seriously?"

"Six murders over a thirty-year period by the looks of it. There's an open investigation into them, ongoing. Has been for a while. Probably stalled out for lack of leads.

The congresswoman was number one, and number six was just three years ago." Geoff paused. "In your neighborhood, actually."

"In my town?"

"No, Portland."

Wyatt rolled his eyes. Of course someone from the East Coast would think Portland and a small town hours away were the same "neighborhood."

He stretched. "A serial killer, really?"

"Exactly." Geoff sounded baffled. "Listen, you want a copy of these files? I can let the agent in charge of the case know you were asking."

Wyatt bounced the idea around in his mind, but all he could think of was Nina's beaten and bruised face. Those big blue eyes looking up at him, tear filled and asking for help.

"Send me everything."

A serial killer.

Was it possible Nina was exactly right, that Mr. Thomas had killed her mom…and then killed five more people over the years? Dread settled over him. She'd faced down Mr. Thomas just yesterday, tangled with a *serial killer* and fought him off sufficiently enough that he'd left her and retreated.

But had he, really?

Wyatt had seen a lot of awful things in his time as a cop and as a marshal. There wasn't a lot that surprised him about what people could do to each other for money, or power, or some misguided sense of love or devotion. But the idea that Nina had been alone with a killer drew a lump into his throat.

He threw on some clothes, not even bothering to check whether his tie matched the rest of it. When he trailed back out of the bedroom, his inbox had a new email from Geoff with multiple attachments.

Wyatt's cousin had flagged the most recent file. Three years ago, a woman—twenty-nine years old—had been found beaten to death in her bedroom. Young daughter. Estranged husband, a soldier, considered a suspect until it became clear he had been deployed at the time. A couple of other suspects, but nothing concrete the investigating detectives could use to get a warrant for anyone's arrest.

More times than he cared to remember, Wyatt had watched the prime suspect in a case walk because of lack of evidence. Despite the fact that every instinct he'd had assured him they were as guilty as a person could get, there had been nothing Wyatt could do about it. Frustrating, to say the least.

He'd have to call the lead detective, though he didn't know what the man's reaction would be. Everyone on the Portland police force thought Wyatt had left for greener pastures. Cops were cops until they died, and they considered it essentially betrayal that he'd transferred to the marshals' fugitive apprehension task force. Either betrayal, or they thought he'd gone because he couldn't handle the job.

Neither of which said much about him that was good.

If Wyatt was going to get anywhere he'd have to call his former partner, a man he hadn't spoken with much in the years since he'd left—despite their being close as brothers. No one except Parker knew the truth of what had happened with his father and the effect it had had on his own career.

But in order to help Nina, Wyatt was going to have to face the past.

* * *

Nina's whole body ached. She blinked away the cloud of sleep and shifted to sit up. She winced and glanced at the door to the hospital room.

Mr. Thomas stood there.

Nina screamed.

Sienna shot from the chair beside the bed and touched her shoulder. "Nina."

Nina blinked. He was gone. "I saw…" She pointed at the door. "He was…"

"Oh, honey." Sienna hugged her and settled on the bed. "It was a flashback."

Nina couldn't stop breathing hard.

"It's completely normal. You had a traumatic experience."

Nina heard what she didn't say, that it had been more than one traumatic experience back-to-back. She squeezed her eyes shut and tried to breathe away the panic the way her counselor had taught her, reciting prime numbers in her head.

Sienna cut in, "Twenty-four, sixty-two. Three hundred and fourteen." A smile infected Sienna's voice.

Nina shoved her away. "You're making me lose count on purpose."

Sienna chuckled. "Want some breakfast?"

"Not really." Nina settled back on the bed. "I'm ready to get out of here."

"Already told the doctor that." Sienna knew how she felt about hospitals, mostly because it was the exact same way Sienna felt. In fact, did anyone seriously *like* being stuck in a bed getting poked and prodded? "He said you should be able to go home this morning."

"Great."

"So." Sienna dragged the word out. "How are you doing?"

"Sore."

Her friend's lips twitched. "I meant about Wyatt."

"I know what you meant." Sienna hadn't hidden her desire to see her friends get together, despite Nina explaining that was impossible.

Was she even ready to talk about the man who had unexpectedly entered her life at possibly the worst moment? "There's no point in talking about it. It's not going to work. Not when I have all this hanging over my head. I have to find the evidence that proves Mr. Thomas was my mother's murderer, and I have to do it before fall semester starts."

Sienna gasped. "You got that job?"

Nina nodded. "They called the day before yesterday."

"And you didn't text me right away?"

"You were at the doctor. Whatever that was about, I didn't want to disturb you." Especially not when it was only a voice mail to say they'd loved her at the interview and wanted her to come in and sign papers.

"But this is huge! Teaching economics at the community college. You'll be here. Settled."

"I know."

"I told you that master's degree would come in handy."

Nina shook her head, smiling. It had been a lot of work, but a student visa had given her a great cover as a CIA agent.

Sienna's eyes were wide, her cheeks flushed. "I get to have you here. Auntie Nina, full time."

"Aunt—"

"I'm pregnant. That's what the appointment was."

"Well, I thought so. I just didn't want to say anything."

Nina grabbed Sienna's hands and held them tight. Her best friend since third grade, her CIA coworker, her family. There was nothing she'd experienced in decades that Sienna hadn't been a part of. "A baby?"

Sienna nodded, her face stretched wide in a smile. "Don't say anything to anyone. I haven't told Parker yet. Things have been a little busy, and I want to find the right moment."

Nina pulled her friend in for a hug. "I'm glad you're happy."

Sienna leaned back. "But you're not, and yet you think somehow that's fine. Because it's not, Nina. You can have what I have, and not when Mr. Thomas has been caught. Now."

She shook her head. "You think he's going to let me be happy? He tried to take me from my apartment. He—" Her voice cracked. Nina swallowed. Blow after blow, not knowing when it would stop and he would drag her off to dump her body in a shallow grave. That would have destroyed Sienna.

"Nina—"

"I think you should go home. I'll call a cab when it's time to leave."

"Why are you doing this?"

Sienna didn't understand, and likely the damage was already done. There wasn't an inch of her life that didn't have Sienna as part of it. Mr. Thomas wouldn't hesitate to use that against Nina. And now with Sienna pregnant on top of everything?

"Call Parker. I'm sure he'll pick you up."

"I drove my car here." Sienna looked like she was about to cry. It was a kick in the stomach when Nina wanted nothing more than to spend the morning with her best friend thinking up possible baby names.

Nina clenched her stomach and looked her friend in the eye. "Please go. I'll be fine."

Because if Sienna was here when Mr. Thomas came around again, she wouldn't be able to guarantee her friend's safety.

Sienna didn't move. "Don't think I don't know what you're doing. Why you're pushing me away all of a sudden." She got up. "I *know*. And if anything happens to you, I'm going to kill Mr. Thomas myself."

Nina didn't smile. "I don't doubt it."

Sienna grabbed her purse and swept out of the room, probably fighting tears. Because Nina was doing the same thing. When the door shut behind her friend, Nina let them come. With tears streaming down her face, she cried out all the fear she'd ever felt for her friend and the worry she had over Sienna's future. And then she prayed.

Everything was finally going right for her friend. Sienna had survived a dangerous career as a CIA agent, amnesia, a fight to the death with bad guys prepared to kill her and a sniper shot to the shoulder. Now she was married and pregnant. Sienna's life had to be safe-guarded. Even if that meant Nina was completely alone for the rest of her life. At least she would know Sienna was safe and happy.

The doctor strode in, took one look at her and said, "Uh…"

She waved off his concern and blubbered through the entire exit procedure. When he left her to get dressed in the fresh clothes Sienna had brought her, Nina cried through that, too.

She wasn't under any illusions that Sienna believed

she could do this alone. Nina knew it would be the hardest thing she ever faced. Mr. Thomas was going to come back for her again. Because there was no way Nina was going to give up this fight.

And neither would he.

That was why she couldn't rely on Wyatt either. She wasn't going to be party to another death. Nina didn't need that on her conscience. Besides, why would Wyatt want someone like her? Nina wasn't a catch. She was a thirtysomething retired CIA agent starting her life over from scratch. All she really had was a bank account—money her parents had left her, plus what she'd earned in the last ten years when she'd had extremely low overhead, sharing a condo with Sienna.

Dollars didn't give her worth, she knew that. But Nina didn't know how to be normal, or how to be around anyone but Sienna. She was getting used to Parker's being part of their lives, but Wyatt was a people person. Nina was only a "Sienna" person. She had been for as long as she could remember. The rest of her life she didn't *want* to remember—she just wanted to be free of it.

Wyatt would expect more of her. And when this business with Mr. Thomas didn't wrap itself up nice and neatly, he would be disappointed.

Nina pulled the shirt on over her sore body and winced. A knock on the door brought her head around. "Come in."

The door opened and Wyatt entered. Nina let go of the breath she'd been holding and grabbed her purse.

"There's no rush. I parked as close as I could to the door without getting in trouble."

"Sorry?"

Wyatt frowned. "Sienna didn't tell you?"

She shook her head. "Tell me what?"

"She asked me to pick you up, said she had something to do this morning."

"I don't need a ride."

"How about a trip to Portland? Are you good for a couple of hours in the car? Because there's something you need to see." He lifted a paper file and waved it at her. "And then we have an interview to do on a related case that might be connected to your mother's murder."

"Are you serious?"

He nodded.

A lead, and she didn't have to go home to her condo and the memories of what Mr. Thomas had done? That sounded like a win-win to Nina. "Let's go."

FIVE

Wyatt pulled up in front of the house and parked. "Her name is Theresa Hammett, seventy-one. Works the checkout at a high-end health food grocer. I called while you were sleeping."

"Sorry about that." Nina brushed hair back from her cheeks. "I didn't get much rest last night."

Why did she feel guilty for having slept on the drive to Portland? He'd been content to listen to the radio and know she was recharging while he drove. It did his heart good, especially since every time he closed his eyes all he saw was Nina on the floor of her condo, unconscious.

"Theresa's here, and she's prepared to talk to us. The investigating detectives haven't gained a new lead on her daughter's murder in months. I didn't mention your personal connection to this, but she knows we're here because of a case that could possibly be linked."

Nina cracked the car door. "The daughter was married?"

Wyatt said, "Divorced, the husband is army. One child, a girl. Emily."

"Same MO."

He nodded. "There are some distinct similarities. That's why it was flagged with your mom's case."

"She was stabbed?"

"Actually, no. It was blunt force trauma to the side of her head that killed her."

So far there was no correlation in the manner of death, only the situation of the murder victim—female, married or recently divorced, one female child. Wyatt was having trouble making sense of any of it. Least of all, how this man—if it really was a serial killer—picked his victims.

"Let's go." He got out his side and came around the car. Nina moved like the drive had stiffened all her muscles, the bruises making themselves known. He'd been in enough fights that he knew what that felt like.

They walked up to the front door side by side while Nina brushed her hair down with her fingers and smoothed out her clothes.

Wyatt lifted his hand to knock, and the door opened. "Mrs. Hammett?"

The woman was five-two with light brown skin, dark hair and eyes, and a trim figure that said clearly she wasn't about to let being in her seventies stop her from doing all the active things she wanted. She smiled at them, not happy, more hopeful and pleasant. Wyatt decided then that she likely had devoted regulars at the grocery store who went in for purchases but stayed for the conversation she offered. She just had that kind of warm demeanor.

"Deputy Marshal Ames?"

He smiled. "Wyatt is fine. This is Nina Holmes, a friend of mine."

Theresa led them to a stylish living room and offered them coffee. When they were all settled with mugs, he asked a few general questions about her daughter. As Theresa's eyes started to fill with moisture, he pulled back and added in questions about the husband.

"He's a good man," Theresa said. "A little hotheaded, but he never crossed any line."

"Why the divorce?"

"Abigail said she fell out of love. Mason was gone so much she felt like they'd stopped connecting. Emily was nine when they split. Not old enough to understand why two people quit loving each other, but old enough to open up about her feelings. Since Abigail's death it's like she closed off. Too much, too soon, I suppose. She may be talking to someone, but it's certainly not me."

Nina reached out and squeezed Theresa's hand. "I'm so sorry for your loss."

Theresa swallowed and nodded. She sipped her coffee and sat back in the chair. "Abigail didn't always make the best choices, but she loved life. She loved her husband well while she did, and treated him well enough when she didn't. Emily was the world to her, so much that it's left Emily adrift without her mother. I try to fill the gap, but what do I know about being twelve?" The smile was gone so fast it was almost a mirage.

Wyatt said, "Can I ask… Was Abigail seeing anyone?"

Theresa nodded. "She kept it pretty secret, but I could see the change. At first I wondered if she wasn't reconnecting with Mason, but when I asked about it she said she'd met someone. It lasted maybe four months before she was killed."

Nina perked up. "Did you ever meet him?"

"No. She had plans to bring him around, but he always had business. After she was killed I never had anyone come by to pay condolences. I kept waiting for a man I'd never seen before to show up at the house and pay his respects." Theresa shrugged. "He never did."

Nina deflated. Wyatt shifted on the couch, tempted to squeeze her shoulder, but he could comfort her later. He knew how important it was to her that she discover Mr. Thomas's real identity.

He asked Theresa, "Abigail's ex-husband, Mason, was originally the prime suspect. What were your thoughts on that?"

"He didn't do it."

"You're sure?"

Theresa wrinkled her nose. "He was deployed. That's why they thought he might have done it. There was a question as to whether he'd managed to get home somehow, for a day, without anyone knowing. I told the police it was ridiculous. They didn't know how he felt about her, how he'd always felt about her. Mason claimed he fell out of love with Abigail at the time they were divorcing, but I never saw it. The way he looked at her?" Theresa shook her head. "He loved her. I think he loved her enough that when she asked for a divorce, he let her go so she could live the life she wanted."

"What made the police change their minds?"

"Emily was adamant Abigail's boyfriend was the one who killed her."

Nina reacted. This story was sounding more and more familiar, though thankfully this time the husband hadn't gone to prison for murder. Wyatt knew from the file that he'd never been charged, since there hadn't ever been enough evidence beyond the fact that Abigail had possibly argued with someone and either fallen, or been pushed, onto the dresser, slamming the side of her head hard enough to kill her.

Nina's back was straight, as though all the muscles had locked in place. "Did the police ever find the man who did it?"

Theresa shook her head. "There was nothing in her house, on her phone, or on her computer that indicated she'd been in a relationship. Emily was the only one who'd seen him, and I'd only heard about him. I didn't even know his name. Abigail never told me. When the police couldn't find him, they didn't know whether to even believe he existed. They wanted to know if Emily was prone to making up stories, as though she'd created him to cover for her father."

Wyatt was going to follow up with the detectives and ask. He'd have likely thought the same thing, though. Especially when there was no physical evidence a person even existed, only the word of a traumatized child whose mother had died. "Is there anything else you can think of that might help us find out who it was that Abigail was seeing?"

Nina glanced at him, and he knew what she was thinking. But the child, despite living here, wasn't present. When he'd called ahead, Theresa had told him she was sleeping over at a friend's house for the weekend. Wyatt had figured that was a big part of why they were there, Theresa trying to shield Emily from any more trauma.

Nina wasn't going to get an interview with the kid. As much as he wanted to help her, Wyatt wasn't going to let her push just because she wanted results. They'd have to figure this out the right way, and not by barreling over people's lives and emotions. Her own mother had been killed and her father framed. He got that she wanted answers more than anything and that she didn't have a whole lot to lose by following through. Especially when Mr. Thomas had paid her a visit.

Maybe he could convince her to let him finish out the investigation on his own. Mr. Thomas didn't need to know. He'd only see that Nina was leaving it alone. Then she'd be safe, and he could find the answers for her.

The front door swung open. All three of them turned to see a slim African-American preteen stride in. "Gramma! I'm home!"

Nina stood. The twelve-year-old had long, curly brown hair and big almond eyes. In ten years she was going to be a knockout with a deceased mother and an absent father. If Theresa wasn't careful, this girl was going to lose her way big-time. Nina was going to add the girl to her prayer list.

Emily set her hand on her hip. "What is this? What's going on?" She glanced through Nina and Wyatt to her grandmother.

Theresa stood. "Honey, what happened at Shanelle's?"

"Vanessa and Trish were colossal jerks so I rode my bike home."

"Honey, you should have texted me."

"I was so mad I needed a time-out, Gramma."

Nina felt her lips twitch. Had she ever had this much presence or attitude? The girl was a spitfire, that was for sure. Nina was a little less worried about her now.

"So what's going on?"

Wyatt stepped forward. "I'm Deputy Marshal Ames. You can call me Wyatt. This is Nina Holmes."

"Not a marshal?"

Nina shook her head. "I was a CIA agent."

The girl's eyes flashed wide. "Seriously, a CIA agent?"

"I'm retired now, but yes."

"Epic."

Nina laughed. Wyatt's low, manly chuckle sounded like a rumble. She glanced at Theresa and saw the resigned look on her face, then stepped forward. "Would it be okay if I talked to you?"

"About my mom?"

"How did you know that?"

The girl shrugged. "What else would it be?"

Nina waved in the direction of the couches. "Would you sit with us, Emily?"

The girl dumped her purse on the hall floor and strode over. "Sure. Whatever. Can I take a selfie with you and put it on Instagram? All my friends will be so mad I met a CIA agent."

"No. Sorry."

Emily shrugged. "Worth a try." She slumped into the armchair opposite her grandmother, and Wyatt and Nina both took their seats again. "What do you want to know?"

Nina led in, asking the girl where she had been when her mom was killed—staying at her gramma's that night—and how she'd come home from school to find her mom. Her dad's face when they had told him had been the hardest part for Emily. Then Nina asked her the best thing she remembered about her mother, and the favorite thing they would do together.

After Emily relaxed, Nina got down to the serious stuff. "The police report includes a statement that you made about your mom's boyfriend at the time. Can you tell me about him?"

Emily's nose wrinkled, almost an exact copy of her grandmother's face. "He was older, and he always wore a suit. At least the couple of times I saw him."

Nina held her reaction in. If this girl could help her figure out who Mr. Thomas was, they would be one step closer to finding and catching him. "What did he look like?"

"His hair was gray, with only a sprinkle of black. He had a square white face. Blue eyes. Some lines on his face." Emily glanced to the side, like she was remembering. "Veins stuck out on the back of his hands, and they weren't rough like Dad's. He wasn't anything like Dad. He had money. We went to an expensive restaurant, and I had to wear a dress." She made another face. "But he was nice. Not really friendly, just pleasant. Snooty."

"Did he say what he did for work?"

"Something business. That's probably not helpful."

"It's great, Emily," Wyatt said. "You're doing fine."

Nina said, "May I ask what made you so sure that he was the one who killed your mother?"

Emily shrugged. "I just knew. Who else would have done it? He spent all that time with her, acted like he liked her. But people say they feel things they don't all the time. Why not lie? He gets what he wants, and then when he's done he kills her."

Theresa gasped, her hand over her mouth.

Nina swallowed. "I was younger than you when my mother was murdered. A lot younger. My father was sent to prison, but I never believed he did it. There just wasn't that much feeling between them. He didn't care enough about her to kill her."

"So who did?"

Nina didn't answer that. Instead she said, "What was his name?"

"Mr. Thomas." Emily stared at her. "Is he the one who did that to your face?"

Nina didn't move. "Yes."

Emily didn't move either, and no one said anything. Finally Nina broke the silence. "There are others he's killed. Or so we believe. But your mother and mine were both murdered by a man in a suit who called himself Mr. Thomas. And I'm going to catch him."

"How?"

"I don't know yet."

"Who is he?"

"I don't know that yet either."

Emily didn't look too impressed, and Nina didn't blame her. They didn't have a lot to go on, at least not until the crime lab was done testing for fingerprints he might have left at her house. Then they'd have to come back with an identity on the print. She and Wyatt had driven three hours to the city of Portland, and for what? Emily had corroborated what Nina knew: the cases were linked.

So, what next?

Wyatt said, "Is there anything else you can tell us that might help us figure out who Mr. Thomas was? Where he lived, what kind of car he drove, anything."

Emily tilted her head one way, then the other. "I can look back through my photos. Like from my phone. They're on my computer now, but I'll see if I remember anything." Her eyes were wet.

"Thank you, Emily. That's a really good idea."

The girl was sharp, and Nina said a quick prayer of gratitude that she'd been nine and not six. A nine-year-old who apparently had a cell phone she took pictures with.

Nina stood. "You've really helped us, Emily. Thank you." She turned to Theresa. "And thank you for your time. If you think of anything else, would you let me know?"

Theresa nodded and stood. "I'll give you a call if Emily remembers anything."

"We appreciate that." Wyatt shook her hand. He followed Nina to the door, putting his hand on the small of her back again. Could he read that she wasn't all that anxious to leave? Still, the injuries Mr. Thomas had given her before the marshals chased him off were sore, and she needed food and another painkiller if she was going to make it through the rest of the day. Her head was pounding.

"You know, there is someone else you should talk to." Nina turned back and Theresa continued, "Abigail's best friend, Ronnie. The police interviewed her, and I don't know if she knew anything. But she might." Theresa gave Wyatt the woman's information.

"Thank you." Wyatt opened the door and let them out.

As they walked to the car, he glanced at her.

Nina bit her lip. "I was right."

He stopped beside her at the car. "You were. So was Emily. He came to your house to try and silence you."

"Mr. Thomas killed my mother, he killed Emily's mother. He came after me. Will he come after them, too?"

"I'm going to call someone about that." Wyatt set his hand on her shoulder. "I'll have the police keep an extra close eye on Emily and Theresa to make sure they're safe."

"Okay." She pushed out a breath. "I don't want him to kill anyone else."

"He won't."

"How can you be sure, Wyatt? He's crazy enough to try and drug and abduct me so he could kill me. Now we know he's basically a serial killer, and we're onto him. We know what he's been doing all these years. We're going to figure it out. He's got to be running scared. That makes anyone unpredictable."

"Nina, he won't hurt you because I won't let him."

Wyatt's phone rang. He pulled it from his back pocket. Nina saw the screen. *Dad*. Wyatt groaned deep in his throat and slid the phone back in his pocket. "Let's go."

SIX

Wyatt saw the look she gave him when he dismissed the call from his dad, but he didn't want to talk to his old man. Not to mention if Nina didn't want to talk about the text, why should he share his issues with his father? As much as he wanted it to be otherwise, they didn't trust each other fully. Not yet.

Wyatt pulled away from the curb in front of Theresa and Emily's house. He used the car's Bluetooth to call his old partner. It rang twice, and the man picked up.

"Well, well, well. Wyatt Ames." The tone of Karl Frank's voice echoed loud and clear through the car speakers. Not happy and not prepared to let Wyatt get away with not talking about it.

He was a career police detective, and they'd been good friends. Once. They still could be, but both were far too stubborn to make the first move. This was just business.

"Don't give me that," Wyatt said. "It's not like you've called me either."

"A man won't, when his partner of six years quits his life just to go be a big shot with the marshals."

Instead of a retort, Wyatt explained the so-far pretty long story of Theresa and Emily.

"So you're here? In Portland?"

"I need a patrol car on regular drive-bys of their house. Keep an eye out."

"Done," Karl said. "But you're here, and not in that Podunk little town?"

"Yes." Wyatt sighed, trying to ignore Nina's staring at him like he had two heads as she listened to the conversation. "We're here in Portland."

"We?"

"Karl." Wyatt saw Nina's lips twitch out of the corner of his eye. "Fine. The woman I told you about, Nina. She's here with me."

"Great. I'll call Tashi. Dinner's at six. Don't bring anything, or she'll get mad."

He hung up.

Nina erupted into giggles. She groaned and circled her arm around her waist, but kept laughing. "That was hilarious."

Wyatt felt the noise of displeasure all the way down in his throat. "Karl is…"

"Yeah, I noticed that." Nina smiled. "I guess we're going to dinner before we go back home?"

"Actually, I was thinking we could interview Ronnie before the end of the day."

Nina motioned to the digital dash clock with one finger. "It's already four."

"I guess maybe we could get a couple of hotel rooms tonight and see if we can interview Ronnie tomorrow? I'll call her next."

Nina nodded, her lips still curled up. "We don't have fresh clothes or toothbrushes."

"This is a city. They have stores. And I don't know why you think this is so funny."

"It strikes me that maybe this Karl guy, your old partner, might be a lot like Parker, your current partner. You think that's a coincidence?"

Wyatt glanced at her, one eyebrow raised. "That I get partner after partner who thinks he's the boss and he knows what's right?"

Nina shrugged, all innocence. "Maybe."

"I don't know what to say about that. It's not like I attract a certain kind of partner. They're assigned."

Nina shifted gently in her seat so she faced him more. "What made you quit the police force and join the marshals?"

Wyatt pulled up at the stoplight. "Technically it wasn't quitting. I still hold the rank of detective, since it was a transfer. First they attached me to the team, then when I was sworn in as a marshal they assigned me to Parker as partner. That was four years ago."

"And you like being a marshal better than being a cop?" She hesitated, so he waited for her to finish. "Sienna said your father was a cop."

"I also have a cousin who's an FBI agent. That's who gave us the tip about Theresa and Emily's case." He paused, but she was probably still waiting for an actual answer to his question. "Yes, I like it better. It's simpler, in a weird way. We already know they're guilty, we just have to bring them in."

"That's it?"

"Why should it be complicated? The investigation's been done. All we have to do is bring them in to face justice."

Wyatt found the drive-through to a coffeehouse he'd visited regularly on his beat as an officer in the Portland police department. Hopefully their joe was still good, because he needed a serious jolt of caffeine if he was going to face Karl and Tashi for dinner.

They were going to ask questions, and Wyatt didn't know if he had the answers. At least not ones that wouldn't birth a whole lot more questions. He'd moved on, and in the process—unfortunately—that meant leaving them behind. They'd been his best friends, but too much had happened. Wyatt had needed the distance and the headspace to deal with bad case after bad case that had left him burned out.

The marshals' service had been a breath of fresh air at a time he desperately needed to breathe.

He turned to Nina. "Coffee?"

"Yes." She sounded as desperate as he felt. Wyatt took the turn smiling.

Nina's phone buzzed. She jumped almost clear out of her seat, flipped the phone over and stared at it. After a few seconds she tapped the screen and read the message.

"Everything okay?" Maybe a relaxing dinner with friends would be good. For her, at least. It would get her mind off Mr. Thomas's reach.

She exhaled. "Yeah, it's just Sienna checking in. I'll call her later." She tapped out a message in response. "I keep thinking it'll be him, messaging me again." She pressed her lips together for a second. "Every time it vibrates it reminds me of that message outside the courthouse."

Wyatt pulled up outside the coffeehouse. "I didn't know how to tell you this before, and I'll preface it by saying this was Sienna and Parker's grand idea and I was against it."

Nina frowned.

"You don't need to worry about messages from Mr.

Thomas because Sienna cloned your phone while you were in the hospital. She's seeing everything you see."

"You didn't say anything." Nina paused. "Is this because I didn't tell you straightaway about the first text? I was nearly run over! I wasn't thinking, except that I'd nearly died. I actually forgot about it until you showed me in the hospital."

"I'm not trying to punish you for forgetting. I said I was against the idea to clone your phone. That was all Sienna."

Nina's gaze didn't move from him. "I thought I told you."

"I remember you looking at your phone. What I'm saying, very badly apparently, is that you're not alone in this." He sighed. "Let's just go get that coffee."

Nina stood in the doorway facing a slender Asian woman with a wide smile. "Thank you for inviting us, Tashi."

The woman made a *pfft* sound with her lips. "I wouldn't have it any other way."

Wyatt stepped forward. "Tashi." She grabbed him and hugged his diaphragm with her fingers locked behind his back until he grunted. "I see nothing has changed."

He'd briefed Nina over coffee on Tashi and Karl Frank while they wandered through a superstore for a change of clothes and toiletries. The couple had been married six years, no kids—though not for lack of trying.

Tashi leaned back and laughed what could only be described as a cackle. Nina smiled. He'd briefed her on that, too. "Come in, come in. Why are you standing in the doorway?"

Karl stepped into the hall. "You heard the woman."

Wyatt stiffened. When Karl strode over they grabbed hands and did that "man hug" thing, which involved a lot of backslapping that made Nina wince.

"Long time." Karl surveyed Wyatt's face. His former partner was older, but on top of it Karl had that air of someone who had seen too much, who knew too much. "Probably not long enough, far as you're concerned."

"I'm here, aren't I?"

Karl motioned to Nina with a tilt of his chin. "And you brought a friend." A pleasantness dropped over him like he'd shrugged on a coat. It put her immediately at ease. "Nina?"

She nodded and shook his hand. They had to see the awkwardness between her and Wyatt. But why was that her fault? It turned out they'd both been keeping things from the other. Though apparently all of it was enough to make him…switch off. Or whatever had happened. She didn't understand it.

She understood covert operations, not people's emotions.

"Come and sit at the table." Tashi waved them in. "I made your favorite."

Wyatt's favorite turned out to be chicken and roasted potatoes. Dinner was more enjoyable once Nina relaxed a bit. These were Wyatt's friends, and she didn't want to make him look bad or be embarrassed. She went at it like this was a CIA operation—only the mission was to be the woman she wanted to be. A funny, chatty, at-home woman about to start teaching college economics in a few weeks.

And it worked. At least until Karl said, "So, Wyatt. Have you spoken to your dad lately?"

Wyatt halted his fork two inches from his open mouth.

He looked like he was about to growl. Tashi, who'd previously been smiling at Nina, turned to both of them and sighed.

"Guess that's a no." Karl shoved in a forkful of broccoli and chewed with an unashamed smile on his face.

Wyatt set his fork down, sat back and folded his arms. "We can't have one meal without you bringing it up, can we?"

Nina glanced between them. They were entering uncharted territory—that much was clear. Too bad she had no idea what this was about other than the fact that Wyatt had ignored his father's call earlier.

Karl lifted his hands. "Who's bringing it up? I'm just saying…"

"What?"

Tashi had evidently had enough, because she said, "He wants to see you." Karl's face whipped around to his wife, but she waved him off. "What? He does."

Karl's eyes narrowed. "You spoke to him?"

"He was at church on Wednesday night." Tashi stared at her husband, dead straight, no backing down.

"When I was working," Karl said. "And you didn't tell me?"

"It's not a secret, it just wasn't notable." Tashi folded her arms, much like Wyatt. "I saw him across the room. When I was getting coffee he did the same—"

"Ambush," Wyatt muttered under his breath.

"That wasn't it." Tashi sighed again. "He asked how I was." She shot her husband a look. "How *you* are. He also expressed an interest in Wyatt's well-being. I asked how he is, and he said, 'Better.' So there." She stood. "I'm going to refill the iced tea."

Tashi strode from the room. Karl's gaze moved to

Wyatt, and Nina felt like the odd man out at the interplay among three people who clearly cared about one another, but weren't all that sure how to show it.

Despite what it might mean that Wyatt's father wanted to talk to him—and Wyatt's reaction to that news—Nina figured it was likely the same issue that existed between the two of them.

For so long it had been only Nina and Sienna. To give and receive love had been simple, their being friends for so long and understanding each other so deeply. Now she struggled over how to navigate that with additional people. She'd never been required to care about anyone but Sienna before. Emotions, sympathy, empathy. None were particularly helpful to a spy who had to complete the mission at all costs. It felt strange that she even *wanted* to learn how to care about him—to feel more than attraction.

Would he reciprocate? Did she want to try if there was a possibility he might brush off her emotions? That would be a disaster, and not the first time someone she wanted to get in a relationship with had responded with a resounding *no*.

Not that she was there with Wyatt. Yet, at least. There was still way too much going on with Mr. Thomas, and now Emily and Theresa. She prayed they would be safe, that Mr. Thomas wasn't watching closely so soon after he'd been in her apartment.

Wyatt touched her shoulder, a gentle smile on his face. Or was that relief? "You look exhausted. Let's head to that hotel."

"Hotel?" Tashi set the iced tea on the table. "No way. Both of you can stay here."

"Tash—"

"Don't you argue with me, Wyatt Ames. I'll tell your girl about the time when you were a beat cop and you tried to—"

Wyatt shot up out of his chair. "Okay, we'll stay."

Tashi sat, a satisfied smile on her face. "She gets the guest room, you get the couch."

Wyatt squeezed her shoulder. "I'll get our bags."

Nina nodded.

As soon as he was out of earshot, Tashi leaned across the table. "Okay, so maybe he seems a bit like a joker, a player even. But he's not. I know that man, and it's all fluff on the surface, no big deal. But Wyatt feels deeper than nearly everyone I know, or have ever met. When he loves, he loves so strong that when it goes bad it almost destroys him, so now he runs from it like he's trying to guard his heart. We don't have long, so I can't go into detail, but trust me on this. It's all shallow on the surface, but it's to protect himself from getting hurt. But for the woman who teaches him how to *believe* in love—" she pointed at the door "—that man will give everything he has to make it forever, and the best she will ever know."

Nina heard his boot steps approach the open front door. "And you think that's me?"

Tashi sat back. "I think it could be."

Out the corner of her eye, Karl glanced between them. "I'm sorry, are you talking about *Wyatt*?"

"What about me?" He strode into the room.

"Nothing." Tashi shook her head, the picture of innocence. "Just girl talk."

Nina smiled. Tashi's warning, or advice, or whatever it was, had poured over her like a fountain. Nina needed a week just to process it all, but Wyatt was right there.

The man Tashi had known wasn't the man Nina met

after her abduction. She'd heard stories of his dating history, but that was all old news. In the months since they had met he'd been…subdued. She didn't think it was because of her, not when it was probably more about his father.

Nina stood. "Thank you so much for dinner. It was amazing."

A smile curled up the corners of Tashi's elegant mouth.

Wyatt handed over her purse. "This was beeping in the hall."

Nina rummaged and pulled out her phone. It was a new text, from the… "Baltimore public library," she breathed.

Wyatt tapped the screen, his shoulder right beside her. The message loaded, an image. A photo of the very preteen they'd met just that morning, along with the words *Emily was never as sweet as my Little Mouse.*

SEVEN

"He's outside her house. We have to go."

Wyatt stared into Nina's earnest eyes and knew she was right. But Mr. Thomas was fixated on her, and Nina was disregarding that because she had to check on Emily. Wyatt figured that "mission ready" attitude was part of her—and probably also a coping mechanism.

Karl paced his living room and barked orders into his phone the way he did when he was trying to down-play his fear.

He touched Nina's shoulder. "Karl and I will go. Stay here with Tashi."

Karl hung up. "The unit outside isn't responding, so they're sending another. They'll arrive on scene before us, but we can meet them there."

"Nina—" She had to be mad he didn't want her there. But when Wyatt glanced at her, she bit her lip.

"Go. Make sure Emily is fine."

He looked at Tashi, but pointed at Nina. "She stays here."

Tashi grinned, but nodded. The woman was ex-military, and now a nurse. But that more distant part of her past hadn't come up in conversation. Nina likely figured if she was going to try something she had to get past a nurse. Not a soldier.

Wyatt returned Tashi's nod.

Outside Karl clicked the locks on his car and they got in. Karl pulled out of the driveway, a grin on his face. "Just like old times."

"Just drive." Wyatt looked out the window at familiar streets that flickered past as Karl tore across town. "Dinner was probably a mistake."

"You don't have to worry. Tashi will take care of her, you know that."

Wyatt flipped his phone over and over on his knee. "This girl is twelve, and the guy is a suspect in a series of murders."

Karl shot him a look. "Okay, so maybe I shouldn't have brought that up, about your dad. You probably haven't told your *friend* Nina about any of that. But—if you don't mind me saying—"

"Like it'd stop you if I did mind."

"Anyway, I'm just saying if this is what your reaction is, maybe there's something still there. I'm guessing you haven't been back home." Karl paused long enough to assess Wyatt's face. "We were partners for years. I know you, Wyatt. You couldn't deal with that last case. You couldn't deal with what happened to your dad. And you *ran*."

Wyatt lifted his phone. So what if he'd found a job that suited him way better, even if his new partner was almost an exact copy of his old partner. It had to be some kind of comeuppance, payback for something he'd done.

"I have to make a call."

Karl snorted. "Sure you do. *Running*."

Wyatt ignored and dialed. Two rings and Parker picked up.

"Sienna saw the message. I ran a trace, and the phone it originated from is on. We pinged the closest cell tower. It's in Juneau, Alaska."

Wyatt blinked at the bright lights of an oncoming car. "What?"

"That's what it says. Are you at Theresa and Emily's house yet?"

"Two streets away. How is he in Alaska and also taking pictures of Emily in Portland?"

"Good question," Parker said. "But that's what the techs tell me." He paused. "So how was dinner?"

Wyatt's stomach churned. He really shouldn't have checked in earlier and told Parker what they'd be doing that night, but he'd figured Sienna would worry about her friend if he didn't.

"You need to tell him."

Wyatt clenched his back teeth together. It had taken two years, but Parker had worn him down. The end of a long weekend, work that had tired them both out so far beyond exhaustion they couldn't fall asleep they'd been so wired. Parker had poked and prodded, and Wyatt had broken down. He'd explained the real reason why he'd made the transfer.

"I'm serious, Wyatt. You should tell him."

"I know that."

"But are you actually going to do it?"

Wyatt was silent. Probably Karl had figured it out, and then they'd be talking about it for no reason whatsoever.

"That's what I thought."

Karl pulled up outside Theresa's house, still eyeing

Wyatt as though he'd very much like to know what he was talking about.

"Gotta go." Wyatt hung up and got out.

Tashi covered Nina's hand with hers. "I'm sure everything will be fine. It was probably nothing but a scare tactic."

Nina shot her a sardonic smile. "I'm officially scared."

Click. The living room blanked into darkness. Not one single light remained.

Nina gasped. "He cut the power." She grabbed her cell from her back pocket and illuminated the screen. *No signal.* She turned it around to shine through the room.

Tashi grabbed her hand. "Get under the dining table. Now."

Before she could ask why Tashi had made that declaration, Nina was shoved toward the archway that led to the dining room. Tashi raced from the room so quietly it rang like bells in Nina's head. Who was this woman? Nina put her hands out, using the dim light from the phone so she could see where she was going.

It had to have been Mr. Thomas who'd cut the power. And done something to her phone.

Her fingers hit the chair back and bent. Nina winced and started to shift the chair aside. Tashi touched her arm, and Nina jumped. She pressed the cold metal of what felt like a revolver into Nina's hand.

"He cut the landline, too. Now hide. And dim that light. I'll cover you."

Theresa was on the porch, her arm around Emily. They were crowded by uniformed police officers, most of whom he thankfully didn't recognize. He strode straight to the two women. "How are you both?"

Theresa nodded, looking understandably confused about the fuss. "We're okay. Thank you." She shifted Emily from under her arm. "Why don't you go inside and put on some coffee for these nice officers, honey?"

"Sure." Emily rolled her eyes, but did as her grandmother asked. "I'm not done looking through my pictures anyway."

When Emily was out of earshot, Theresa said, "How worried should I be that this murdering freak is going to come around my granddaughter again?"

Wyatt thought about Nina, back at Karl's house with Tashi. "A healthy worry is never a bad thing."

With Tashi. At Karl's house.

Mr. Thomas wasn't here now, and they'd left Nina there. He couldn't have known Wyatt and Karl would do that. He couldn't even know they'd planned to stay the night in Portland.

Right?

The retort of gunfire flashed like lightning through the dark house. Tashi cried out.

Nina prayed Tashi had fired, or if she hadn't that she wasn't hurt. Or not hurt too badly. *Lord, what's happening? Help us.*

The time for hiding was over. Nina lifted the revolver Tashi had given her and aimed the phone's flashlight in her other hand along with it. The injuries Mr. Thomas had given her last time ached, but at least he hadn't broken her ribs. Just bruised. Still, she didn't want to be in another fight anytime soon.

Had Mr. Thomas drawn the men away for this reason?

Pretending to target Emily to get Nina on her own, or exposed? So he thought. Tashi could hold her own, that was for sure. *Please, Lord.*

Nina crept down the empty hall to where Tashi had been positioned. Where the shots had come from. She gripped the butt of the gun and the phone, scanning as she went. Nina couldn't risk not seeing where the threat was coming from until it was too late.

Where was Wyatt? Was he heading back? Had he sent officers ahead to help them? Hopefully Emily and Theresa were fine, because Nina thought maybe Tashi might not be. Her phone started to ring.

Baltimore Public Library.

She should end the call and dial Wyatt's number, but would it go through when the phone still registered no signal? Mr. Thomas was trying to throw her off.

"I'm not going to answer that. Why don't you come out so we can talk?" She stepped closer to Tashi's position. Nina was supposed to be hiding under the dining table. Like that was going to happen when Tashi could be injured.

"Why talk?" His voice made her shudder. "All you need to do is die…like your friend here." He spoke slowly, a smooth tone that held no happiness, no sadness. It just was. And it made her want to rage. "All that warm blood seeping onto the carpet. Whatever will she do? Gasping for breath. Will help come before she expires?" His chuckle was high-pitched, insane.

Nina's phone quit ringing. She swiped at the screen and emergency-dialed 91—

Two arms banded around her waist and lifted her feet off the ground. The gun dropped to the floor, along with her phone. He dragged her backward, and the pain from her ribs stopped her from taking even a partial breath. She gasped, tried to scream.

White spots blinked in the corner of her eyes like lightning bugs.

He hauled her back with him. Where were they going? This wasn't how things were supposed to end. Nina pried at his fingers, his hot breath on her hair. She kicked at his legs, but couldn't hit anything. Strength bled from her the way he said Tashi's blood was doing right now.

Wyatt and Karl had left her with Karl's wife, and now both of them would die, and it would be all Nina's fault.

The animosity between the two men would snap and break like a rubber band stretched too tight. They would never speak to each other again. That was, as long as they didn't kill each other instead.

Sometimes there was only one way to get rid of the pain, and that was to expunge it out of your system. Nina had seen it happen many times—people stuck where they didn't want to be. The world was a messed-up if not downright evil place to live. She'd met men, women and children imprisoned in a life no one should have to live.

Sometimes there was only one way out, and it wasn't cutting yourself off the way Wyatt had done.

Her hip clipped a counter, and his arms loosened. Nina sucked in a breath and screamed. He hit her head with a solid object and she went down on her hands and knees. A rush of cold air hit her.

He dragged her outside.

"No, I'm not!" Tashi yelled. Why was Tashi yelling? "He shot me! I don't know, but Nina needs help, and you better not be late!"

She sounded angry more than in pain. But that didn't

mean this might not very well be almost the end for Nina. They hadn't won yet, and neither had Mr. Thomas.

He pulled her by the arm, but Nina stumbled. Mr. Thomas dropped his shoulder and it hit her stomach. She folded over his back, and he hiked her up and strode away like it was no big deal to walk with a person on his shoulder.

Nina batted her fists on his back and screamed. She kicked her legs and pummeled his stomach with her knees, but it wasn't enough. He was going to carry her off to her death.

She fought harder. There was no way.

She liked her life. She wanted to teach. She wanted more coffees with Wyatt, but without the awkwardness of today. If she gave up there would be none of that. *Give me strength, Lord. I have none.*

With a roar, Nina renewed her fight. She heard him grunt. "I'm not going to let you kill me. Enough is enough." She'd woken up now, and like a mama bear she was mad. "You won't kill me like you killed all those other women. If you hurt Tashi, I'm going to shoot you for it."

He chuckled. "You dropped your gun."

The wail of sirens approached the house.

The outside air was cool, but she didn't care. The low temperature invigorated her to keep trying. There was nothing that would stop her now. Nina wasn't ever going to give up.

He shifted her on his shoulder and gripped the back of her legs as his other arm came across the back of her knees. She was going to fall off. And now she couldn't even kick him!

"Let. Me. Go!"

More sirens.

They were almost at the back of Karl and Tashi's mammoth yard now, walking through a raised bed with corn stalks brushing across her face. Mr. Thomas had probably parked on a street that backed up to theirs. He would carry her off to his white van, and she'd be nothing but evidence. A lengthy report, the sad tale of a woman who wouldn't let her mother's murder go and the killer who came back to finish the job.

Well, he'd picked the wrong woman when he had shown up at her house all those years ago.

Nina struggled, slammed her fists on his back and roared.

A door slammed.

She lifted her head. "Wyatt!" She screamed his name at the top of her lungs.

Mr. Thomas's steps faltered. He tossed her, and she landed on the grass on her behind with a grunt. Where was her weapon? She had nothing.

He was going to kill her now, and there was no way she could fight him off when he was bigger and stronger.

But someone did have a gun. "WYATT!"

The glint of a knife flashed in the moonlight. She couldn't see his face, but did that matter? In a minute she would take her last breath, a statistic. A memory.

His hand gripped her hair and pulled her face back to his. "What did you just say?"

"Wyatt," Nina breathed.

"Well. This just got a lot more interesting. I suppose that was the man in your condo? Did you tell him all about me?"

"So what if I did?" she gasped.

"Then he must die, too."

"No—"

Mr. Thomas lifted the knife above her chest.

Nina squeezed her eyes shut. But she never felt it slice into her. Instead a gunshot echoed across the yard.

She opened her eyes in time to see Mr. Thomas running away, holding his arm.

Wyatt.

Everything went black.

EIGHT

Her face was pale, with dark circles under her eyes. The bandage on her temple had been placed there by EMTs after Wyatt fired his gun and scared Mr. Thomas away. That knife. He'd foregone thought and simply fired in an attempt to save her life. But Mr. Thomas had seen Wyatt, and the shot had gone wide.

When he'd reached her, Nina had been lying alone at the end of the yard, unconscious. She'd refused to go to the hospital, and instead Nina spent the night on Karl and Tashi's couch with Wyatt sitting in the armchair across from her because she didn't want to be alone. When she wasn't waking because a phone rang, wondering if it was news about Tashi's condition, Nina woke in a cold sweat, convinced Mr. Thomas was back.

If Mr. Thomas had intended to get Wyatt out of the way so he could scare Nina half to death, mission accomplished. But he'd been there to kill her.

The vibrant woman Wyatt had met weeks ago was now subdued, jumpy and constantly looking over her shoulder.

Last night had been her third run-in with Mr. Thomas and his twisted agenda of terror. Despite her determination to see this through to the end, she was doing so with less verve this morning.

Wyatt set his coffee on the dinner table and lifted his phone.

"No news?" Her voice was soft.

Wyatt glanced at her, huddled against the window beside him in the booth, and shook his head. Tashi was still in surgery. She'd been shot twice, once in the thigh and the other—much less serious—across the back of her shoulder as she'd rolled to escape Mr. Thomas. The shoulder wound had taken fifty-six stitches.

Wyatt was more angry than anything else, but they had to keep the appointment with Emily's mother's best friend that they'd made the day before. Neither wanted to miss anything worth knowing about Mr. Thomas. Still, he couldn't help but think there was something Nina wasn't telling him.

Wyatt gripped his coffee cup so hard he worried it might crack. The man had thoroughly played them, and Wyatt hadn't even seen it coming. Sure he'd fired at Mr. Thomas, and it seemed he'd wounded the man. But he was supposed to be protecting Nina, and he'd thought he was until he realized that splitting them up was what Mr. Thomas had intended.

Now Wyatt was going to make sure that Mr. Thomas didn't get to try again.

The protection they had placed on Emily and Theresa had been stepped up and tightened to ensure their continuing safety. All he had to worry about was Nina. And worried was exactly what he was.

"Are you sure you're well enough for this?"

Nina set her own coffee cup down and shot him a look. "Will you stop asking me that?"

Wyatt sighed.

"Any word from Karl now?"

He flipped his phone over on the table. He opened his mouth, but Nina's eyes immediately came alert. She had switched on to some kind of "operator" mode and straightened in her chair. Wyatt looked at the door and saw the best friend of Emily's mother glance around.

He'd looked into her. Ronnie Walters was the mom of three kids, the oldest of whom was about to start high school, but she still had the bearing of a cheerleader. Her husband was a bank manager she'd met in college, and Ronnie cut hair Tuesday through Thursday when her kids were at school.

Wyatt came halfway out of his seat, far enough that she saw him and angled their way. After introductions had been made, she ordered green tea and a slice of whole wheat toast from the waitress. When the food was delivered, Ronnie held the mug in her hands as though the breezy chill of the morning had turned to an early January frost.

"Theresa said you have questions about the man Abby was seeing." Her gaze darted between them and settled on Wyatt. He didn't blame her. Nina was an anomaly in this situation Ronnie probably didn't know how to handle. Wyatt doubted anyone came into her salon bruised up as though they'd been through a war.

Wyatt nodded. "That's right. Anything you can tell us about him will help."

"Because you think he killed her, and that he's killed others, too."

Wyatt nodded again, holding in the surprise that Theresa had shared that much. He sure hadn't.

Ronnie said, "His name was Thomas. But I'm guessing you already know that."

Nina shifted on the seat. "Did you ever meet him?"

Ronnie shook her head, and Nina deflated. Ronnie said, "When Abby finally told me about the new guy she was seeing, it had already been going on for months. *Months.* Can you believe that? She told me he was a very private person, and that he'd asked her not to tell anyone about him, but she did eventually tell me."

Ronnie's face twisted, awash with grief and the betrayal of a deep trust between friends. "Mostly I just figured he was married and that's why he didn't want her to tell anyone. What did I know? It was only a few weeks later she was dead. Emily was at her gramma's for the night, came home after school the next day and found her. Hours and hours my Abby lay on the floor dead and *no one knew.* So you catch this guy, okay? I want him to pay for what he did to my friend."

"What about Abby's husband?" Wyatt fingered his coffee mug. "Didn't the police consider him a suspect at one time?"

"Mason? Not for long. The man's a hothead and a soldier, a workaholic if that's what you want to call it. But he woulda walked through fire for Abby. He never wanted that divorce, but she figured she was giving him the out he never would've asked for. Not when they had Emily. I told them there was no way he did it. He was deployed, and he hadn't sneaked home somehow. He was on an operation. The theory didn't go anywhere."

Ronnie sniffed. "I kind of figured that boyfriend of hers was some kind of hit man hired to kill her and then disappear. The police had no clue who he was, where he went or even where he'd come from." She shrugged slender shoulders. "The police couldn't even figure out if he existed in the first place. Then they started looking at Mason, thinking he hired the hit man. But he was deployed at the time, and he didn't have that kind of money. I've regretted saying it ever since."

"Mr. Thomas exists." Nina's voice was cold.

She'd latched on to one thing Ronnie said—the question of whether Mr. Thomas existed—and responded to it. He'd known she was in the middle of this, not just close to it. She was bypassing facts to focus on her emotion. She wouldn't have made a good cop, but Wyatt figured that wasn't necessarily a character flaw.

Ronnie motioned to Nina's bruised face. "He do that to you?"

"Yes."

"Catch him for me."

"I'm going to."

Wyatt glanced between the two women, not liking at all where this was going. Nina had to be on board with Mr. Thomas's receiving justice, not whatever punishment she deemed appropriate. He wasn't going to stand by and watch, and then allow her to try to explain the mitigating circumstances to whoever was going to be on cleanup duty. The woman was a former spy. She could have killed people in her former life for all he knew.

Before he could lay out some ground rules, Ronnie excused herself. Wyatt glanced at Nina, who bit her lip and looked right back at him. "I'm not going to back down. He'll keep coming after me."

"So go on vacation to Australia for a month." He shifted so he could see her better. "Let me investigate this, and when Mr. Thomas is brought in you can come back."

"You think he won't follow me across the world?" She paused. "I used to think he was some kind of clandestine agent, but I could never prove it. He could be anybody, any*thing*. And he won't stop. The last few days have proven that if nothing else. He cut the power to the house. He was calling me when I had no signal. Sienna got the text about Emily, but she didn't get any calls on the clone, just me. Mr. Thomas has technical skills we can't compete with."

Wyatt nodded. "Fair enough."

"Don't shut me out."

"I won't."

She stared at him a moment longer, then her phone rang. "It's Emily." She answered the call. "Are you serious?" Pause. "Thank you so much."

Nina hung up. "Emily went through her phone, and then her computer. She has an old picture. Of Mr. Thomas."

Nina was no longer the only person who had seen Mr. Thomas close enough to be able to identify him. Wyatt had chased him from her condo, and Emily—and others—had met him as children. He'd shot at the man in Karl and Tashi's backyard.

They strode from the diner, and Nina walked out ahead of Wyatt. Where she was in a hurry to get to, she didn't know. The police were going to email the picture to Wyatt. They should probably be getting home to their own town. She didn't want Mr. Thomas anywhere near Emily, and if Nina could lead him away from the young girl then all the better.

Wyatt caught her hand with his and unlocked the SUV. She didn't look at him. It wasn't that she'd thought he didn't believe her that Mr. Thomas was real. He'd seen evidence. But a picture? They would be able to run the photo through databases that could match his picture to a name. Finally his real identity would be known.

Nina had never been this close before. It was so tangible she could almost taste it.

Wyatt walked her to the passenger side and held the door for her. She frowned at his gentlemanly actions, but he only shrugged. His phone beeped. Before she could ask if that was the picture, he shut the door. When he got in the driver's side he tucked away his phone. "Tashi's out of surgery."

"That's good."

He nodded, a look of relief on his face. "It is."

This time Nina reached over and squeezed his hand. He held hers back and didn't let go. He'd been a rock in the two days since she'd nearly been killed in that hit-and-run, and he didn't seem to be planning to let up anytime soon. Despite being a stubborn, immovable rock at times, he had still helped her. "Thank you."

He glanced over. "For what?"

"Being here. Staying with me." She shrugged. "Everything."

"You're welcome." She saw sympathy, not sure if she entirely appreciated the fact that she needed it. But there was an edge there in his eyes also. An edge she'd seen a few times over the last two days, one that said she was a little too determined to find Mr. Thomas.

She was used to it. The men she'd met her whole adult life had each eventually looked at her that way. At least the ones who'd known she was a CIA agent knew why. She'd gathered intelligence that toppled empires of men determined to rip the world apart for their own selfish gain, men who had to be brought low. And she'd been proud to be part of it. To do her part to make the world better. Safer.

This time she would be the one doing the takedown. This time it was personal. Mr. Thomas had bought that with the way he'd systematically destroyed her family, her solitude and her plan to get justice for both of her parents. Not to mention shooting Tashi.

If Wyatt thought she had a one-track mind, it was because she did. There was no room for these personal feelings that seemed to hover in the air between them. No room for the softness he brought out in her. Nina had to stay the course or risk Mr. Thomas's destroying her completely.

"Home?"

She glanced at him, nodded.

"All righty then."

Nina would have smiled, but only had the energy for a long exhale. Wyatt squeezed her hand and said, "Sleep." According to the clock on the dash it wasn't even lunchtime yet, but Nina didn't argue.

She woke when they pulled into town. Wyatt handed over his phone. He told her the pass code, and she unlocked it to see the photo was onscreen. "That's him." She handed it back, not willing to look at it any longer.

Wyatt tucked the phone away. "Okay."

That was it? *Okay.* Nina didn't know how to respond to that.

As downtown whizzed past, she realized he was headed for her condo. "Actually, could you drop me at Sienna's?" She tried to keep her voice light, and hopefully it worked. Wyatt didn't need to know she was relieved that she hadn't stepped foot in her own place since she'd been there with Mr. Thomas. Or that she had no intention of going back anytime soon.

She pulled out her own phone and sent her friend a text. Sienna would understand, and she'd let Nina sleep on her couch.

Wyatt frowned at her, but changed direction and headed south.

"Sorry, it's probably out of your way."

"It isn't."

She glanced at him.

"I live a quarter mile up the same road. Hang a left at the tree stump."

"The tree stump?"

He shrugged. "It's a dirt track with no street sign. Half a mile up the mountain and you're at my cabin."

In a weird way, it made perfect sense. The boots, the jeans. They weren't just a "look," they were him. "Huh."

"It's not your fancy high-rise, but it's home."

"I'm not—"

He pulled up and parked. "We're here."

Before she could answer, he climbed out of the car. Nina grabbed her belongings from the foot well behind her seat. He'd made an assumption. She hated when anyone did that, let alone when it was a man whose opinion mattered. A lot. He'd seen her condo, noted its price tag and come to a conclusion that put her in a box. A moneyed, snobby box she'd hated basically her whole life. Was it her fault that her parents had amassed some money? It hadn't made their lives better. Private boarding school hadn't made her life better.

While Nina had considered it a blessing she was able to concentrate on the search for Mr. Thomas right now, it wasn't like she was going to lie on her couch all day, every day and eat bonbons while other folks went to their jobs. She had one starting in a few weeks.

Nina stomped past him and let herself in the house.

Sienna came out of the kitchen, wiping her hands on a towel.

"Can I sleep on your couch?"

"I finished the guest room."

Nina changed directions and headed for the hallway. "Even better."

Sienna's gaze was fixed on the doorway, but Nina didn't want to talk to Wyatt or about Wyatt. Not when he thought she was judging him because he didn't have as much money as her. For all she knew, he could be a billionaire who wanted to be a federal agent, and who lived in a cabin because he *liked* it.

Nina slammed the guest room door.

Wyatt turned to leave.

"Not so fast there, buddy."

He glanced over his shoulder at Sienna's raised eyebrow. "It's been a long day."

"You're not going to tell me what that was?"

"I don't know what that was."

"And it didn't have anything to do with why she's here and not at her place?"

Wyatt shrugged. "I'm tired, Sienna."

"Fine, I'll let it go."

She might have, but Wyatt didn't. The question stayed with him on the drive to his cabin. He had no idea what was going on in Nina's head, and it seemed that she didn't have much intention of sharing with him. And why did that bother him so much? He wasn't sure he'd ever cared what a woman thought before—why would he when it would be indecipherable anyway?

Okay, so he wasn't man-of-the-year material. But things with Nina were different. Finally his relationship with a woman had begun with friendship, and he'd thought they were building a foundation from there. Maybe they weren't. Maybe he and Nina were just too different and they'd never find a common ground.

Wyatt's thoughts sputtered like he'd run out of gas. He hit the brake and stopped, eyes on his cabin.

The front door was open.

NINE

Wyatt hit Send on a text to Parker and crept toward his front door, weapon ready. The neighbor lady who cleaned his house had a key, but today wasn't her day. She'd never even so much as left the place unlocked—even though Wyatt did it all the time. He had nothing worth stealing, and she'd never leave the door open anyway.

Entranceway was clear. It wasn't a big place, maybe eleven hundred square feet total, but the layout was like a maze. The blind corners had given him pause when he'd bought it, but he'd figured one day he might need the defensive advantage in his home. *Guess that day is today.*

Kitchen was clear.

Hall. Living room. Same.

The door to his bedroom was wide, so he peered around the corner.

"Don't just stand there, come in."

Wyatt went gun first, just to make the point. "Hands on your head, you're under arrest."

Mr. Thomas turned. "I don't think so." A vicious scratch had left a raw red line from the corner of his left eye down to his jaw.

Wyatt lifted his chin. "Nina do that to you?"

Mr. Thomas's eyes narrowed.

"I said hands on your head."

The man cocked his head to the side. "Hmm. I don't see it."

Was Wyatt supposed to know what he was talking about? The man had broken into his cabin to chat, but Wyatt wasn't going to assume an attack wouldn't be forthcoming.

"Especially considering the 'victim, father' angle." The man's accent was upper class. He likely blended in well at the country club, especially in that tailored shirt and slacks and those loafers. He must have changed after tussling with Nina on the grass the night before.

Wyatt said, "Is that supposed to mean something to me?"

The longer Wyatt could get him to peaceably hang around, the better chance he and Parker had of bringing the guy in without too much hassle. They'd brought down violent criminals before, and if a physical altercation could be avoided, that was preferable. But the man *was* going down. He'd shot Tashi. And while she would recover, Karl was a total wreck.

Wyatt didn't blame him. Thinking Nina might have been hurt, it had felt like his heart stopped beating for a second. He couldn't imagine what Karl was feeling.

Parker hadn't replied, but he would be here in minutes. Wyatt just had to stall.

"I spent the day doing my homework." Mr. Thomas turned slowly. He surveyed the photo frames on Wyatt's dresser, old family pictures. His parents' vow renewal. He lifted a picture of Wyatt and his brother with their arms around their father, the shorter, gray-haired man between them.

"Interesting man, your father. I understand he was a cop, like you. Left the force right around the time you transferred out of the police department. Though I don't blame you, greener pastures and all that." Mr. Thomas paused. "And while I understand his move perfectly well, choosing to resign in the face of what he had to know was coming, I don't so much understand yours."

What his father had coming? The man was making assumptions he knew nothing about. "What it is, is none of your business."

He knew what Mr. Thomas was doing. Or trying to do. It was the biggest angle there was, the most obvious and he was aiming true. He was attempting to get in Wyatt's head and throw him off. But Wyatt knew it, which gave him the advantage. He lifted his gun back up the inch it had slipped. "I'm not going to ask again."

"He's been trying to call you, hasn't he? Guess you have nothing to say. Maybe you feel like he betrayed you, betrayed the brotherhood, his badge. Sacred honor and all."

"Like you could understand any of that."

"Hmm. More than you may think." Mr. Thomas paused for a breath, his words measured as though he had all the time in the world.

Where was Parker?

"I, too, once belonged to a brotherhood. I had a mission, a cause to fight for. They sold that and every one of us bought it. But the rose always withers, does it not? Faith dies. Love fades. Things lose their shine, and all you're left with is the bitter truth."

"And what's that?"

"Nina and I are tied together. We are bonded in a way you cannot even dream of. And you will never, not for all the trying in the world, be able to sever that connection. It was forged in blood, and she will never feel for you what she feels for me, not once in the rest of her life. Me? I made her *free*."

Dread flooded Wyatt like an ice bath on an already cold day, and he clenched his stomach to keep from shivering. This guy was insane.

Mr. Thomas's expression was blank, even with all he'd been spouting. "All you have is guilt you haven't saved her from me. That's not a basis for a relationship, regardless of her deluding herself into thinking she has *feelings* for you. She's not capable of giving you what you want."

"And you know her better than she knows herself, am I right?"

Mr. Thomas didn't answer.

Figures. Wyatt could barely stomach the arrogance pouring off this guy. It was everything he hated about rich people who thought money could buy them out of their problems, their habits or their charges. And yeah, he might have taken that out on Nina when she was clearly different. But he'd seen it so many times he could almost spot it before the person even said anything.

Wyatt stepped forward. "Connection or not, you're under arrest. I'd read the list of charges, but it might take a while." This guy wasn't going to get in his head. Wyatt was no longer prepared to let that happen.

Mr. Thomas lifted his hands to elbow height and held his palms out. That didn't mean he didn't have a weapon stashed somewhere on his person. Wyatt circled around to the back of him. "Hands."

Mr. Thomas moved.

Wyatt blocked the first blow, and the second. He hit back, used his gun as weight and saw Mr. Thomas stumble. He stepped forward, then realized too late that the man had faked it. Mr. Thomas's uppercut hit Wyatt on the chin.

He blinked, stumbled back and shook off the daze. Hit back. Caught him in the stomach. The ribs. Breath whooshed from Mr. Thomas's lungs.

Wyatt reached for a pair of flex cuffs. In the space of a blink, Mr. Thomas's hand darted out. His locked fingers hit Wyatt right in the throat.

Wyatt choked, fell to his knees and gasped for breath. The gun dropped to the carpet.

Air. He needed air.

Where was Parker? Mr. Thomas was getting away. Pant legs appeared in front of him, shoes. Then a cold voice said, "It's time to say goodbye, Wyatt Ames. This has been fun, but now I have more important matters to attend to. Adios."

Wyatt grabbed for the place on Mr. Thomas's arm he thought he'd hit in Karl's backyard.

Mr. Thomas cried out, but managed to punch him again. In the throat. Again.

Wyatt collapsed on the floor of his bedroom, still trying to suck air into his screaming lungs, but curled up enough he could reach his ankle and the backup weapon he kept in a holster there.

He lifted the gun and fired at Mr. Thomas once again as he ran from the scene.

Wyatt coughed, rolled and tried to get up. Collapsed back down. He fumbled for his phone, dropped it.

Message did not send.

He called Parker's number. *Your call cannot be connected.*

Were they okay? Had Mr. Thomas done something to them, or to their house?

It was getting easier to breathe, but he was still likely going to pass out. Before he did, he called 911. It rang. And rang. *I'm sorry, your call cannot be connected.*

Black spots flickered on the edges of Wyatt's vision. He was going to pass out. His friends were in danger.

And there was nothing he could do about it.

From far away, a phone rang. Nina set her mug on the coffee table and turned toward the sound. Not her phone, and despite it being early morning it hadn't woken her. She'd have to have been asleep in the first place for that.

"Are you kidding me?" Parker's heavy steps strode down the hall toward her. "Yes. We'll be there in two minutes."

Nina glanced over the back of the couch where he muttered, "I don't believe this," pulling on his jacket. He glanced up. "Don't just sit there, get dressed." He glanced over his shoulder. "Sienna! Let's go!"

"What happened?"

"Mr. Thomas attacked Wyatt." Nina shot off the couch while Parker continued, "He's at his house and awake enough to explain what happened. I'll meet you there."

Nina looked around for the jeans she'd bought in Portland. "Is he okay?"

"He's alive." Parker shut the front door.

Sienna emerged from the bedroom, and Nina got dressed. Sienna drove them to Wyatt's in her car. Nina didn't even know where his place was, but for Wyatt's description of a tree stump. Apparently Mr. Thomas did, though. What had he done? Why had he turned on Wyatt so soon after they'd returned from Portland?

Dawn had barely broken. Sienna took the curves at a speed that made Nina grab the handle at the top of the door. When she pulled up outside a log cabin, she parked on a grassy bank off to the side of two cop cars, Parker's SUV and an ambulance. The front door was wide open, two cops on the porch.

Nina threw the car door open and raced over. She ran inside and saw Parker at the end of the hall. "Over here." He sent her a chin lift that didn't reassure her one bit.

"How is he?"

"Beat up, having trouble breathing, but alive even though he lay on his bedroom floor hardly breathing for *hours*."

A simple "Okay" wasn't good enough? The man felt it necessary to affirm the fact that Wyatt was alive. Parker's face had paled and his chest heaved with breath until his wife hugged his middle and he visibly relaxed. Parker was reassuring himself that Wyatt was okay, that he was alive. Nina relaxed. That's what was going on—Parker was freaked out because he cared so much for his partner.

She turned the corner and saw him then. Scratches. Bruises. His throat red, raw and swollen. And he'd lain there all night? He hadn't tried to call them? A lump stuck in her throat and she surged forward.

"STOP!"

His barked command made her trip over her feet. She stumbled but remained standing. "What?" He didn't want her near him? Why couldn't she go to him?

His eyes were hard, and the EMT beside him gently felt his throat with gloved hands. Someone pushed at Nina's back, trying to get her to move. The rushing sound in her ears coalesced into words.

"Excuse me."

Wyatt shifted his head to the side and winced. Nina got the message and moved out of the way. A uniformed police officer passed her, carrying what looked like a plastic toolbox.

He scraped under Wyatt's fingernails and closed the implement in its own container, sealing it up in a plastic bag that he wrote on.

"Thanks." Wyatt shook the man's hand.

"You got evidence?" Parker stepped forward so he was beside Nina.

Wyatt nodded. "DNA."

Was he serious? "How?"

Wyatt turned to her. He motioned for her to come to him, but she didn't move. Nina couldn't think past all the questions. "How did you get DNA?"

"Actually, it was you who gave me the idea." His voice was raw. It looked like it hurt to speak. "You scratched him in Karl and Tashi's yard. On his face."

Parker shifted to face her. "We can run that DNA and get an ID. Between that and the photo, we have a decent shot at finding out who this guy actually is."

"He's a killer," she said. "What else do we need to know?"

Parker set his hand on her shoulder. "Once we have his name, the tables turn. We go on offense instead of constantly reacting to whatever he does. You and Wyatt will be out of harm's way."

Sienna said, "Why did he come after Wyatt?"

Nina turned to her friend. It was a good question, but she didn't know the answer.

"Wyatt is connected to this now." Parker's words were measured, cautious.

Nina took a step back anyway. This was her fault. She'd put Wyatt on Mr. Thomas's radar. "First he shoots Tashi, and now he comes after you? I thought everything was directed at me because I'm trying to catch him." It should have been. No one else was supposed to get caught in this killer's cross fire.

"Nina—"

"No." Sienna was going to try and convince her that it was fine when it wasn't. Or that there was nothing she could have done to prevent this. Nina couldn't handle that. Wyatt could have died and it would've been her fault. She fought the urge to go to him, to touch him and reassure herself that he was okay.

The EMT said something. Parker squeezed her arm, then shook Wyatt's hand in some elaborate move she didn't know. Sienna said, "We'll be outside."

And then she was alone with him. He sat on the bed, looking for all the world like he'd been run through one of those old-fashioned clothes dryers that squeezed things flat.

"Come here, Nina."

She didn't move. "The last time I tried to do that, you yelled at me." She didn't mean to sound impatient, but what if she hugged him and wound up hurting him? She was beginning to understand Parker's reaction.

"Because the evidence on me hadn't been collected." He sighed. "Nina, come here."

She made it to him on wooden legs. Wyatt put his hand on her shoulder and used it to keep him stable when he stood. She looked up at his dark eyes and touched his forearm so he didn't break their connection.

Wyatt said, "I'm okay. I tried to arrest him. We fought. I got DNA, and he clocked me in the throat before I tried to shoot him. Then he was gone."

"Is that supposed to make me feel better?"

His face softened and he pulled her to him. Nina wrapped her arms around his waist and fought the tide of emotion that threatened to turn the lump in her throat to tears. Crying never solved anything, even if Sienna said it made her feel better. It didn't change things; it only made Nina's face puffy and blocked her sinuses.

The front of his shirt was warm from his body heat. Maybe she'd tell Sienna about her discovery of how nice it was to be hugged by a man who was taller and stronger than her at a time when she didn't feel good. Though given that Parker was Sienna's husband, she probably already knew that.

Nina pulled in a big breath and sighed, relaxing into the hold Wyatt had on her. "Thank you."

His hand was on the back of her neck as his fingers sifted through her hair. "You're welcome." His chest shook like he was laughing.

Nina leaned back and tried to scowl. "What exactly is funny about this?"

"Plenty." He squeezed the back of her neck and gently pulled her in so her head was back on his chest. "But I'm not done with the hug yet."

"Were you really lying here all night?"

"I was passed out, mostly. Tried to call Parker, didn't get anything. Tried 911. I think he did something to my phone the way he did to yours. I lost track of time. When I woke up enough the phone worked. So I called it in." Wyatt paused. "I'm still trying to figure it all out. My phone log says I called the cops just before midnight, but it never went through. I woke up a little after six and called again. That's when they came."

Nina looked at the alarm clock. "It's eight now."

"I told the cops not to call Parker for a while. I thought the call didn't connect because he was on a job. I wasn't really thinking clearly. But they checked with the office and nothing was going on so they called him."

His phone, lying on the bed, rang. Wyatt pulled her with him as he went to answer it. "Ames." His eyes flashed wide. "You're kidding me. Yes. Yes, I understand. Thank you." He hung up.

"That was Karl. Someone tried to kill Ronnie Walters."

TEN

Nearly killed, and all their fault. Wyatt watched Nina settle in a leather chair in the conference room at the marshals' office. She sipped the coffee Sienna had prepared for her, but didn't meet his eyes. Nina was a pretty good distraction from the fact that they'd shared a meal with two women recently and now both were in the hospital in critical condition.

They'd spent the morning being fed the details in real time. She'd been shot, and the timing fit Mr. Thomas's driving from Wyatt's cabin back to Portland, though it was close. Ronnie's husband had returned home after his early-morning workout at a local fitness club to retrieve a file he'd left there and found his wife bleeding out.

Jonah Rivers cleared his throat. The senior marshal was Wyatt's boss and a good friend. Jonah had been promoted a few months back after the town was flooded and their former boss was killed during a manhunt. Parker had taken his place as team leader, but Jonah still hovered like a mother hen. Wyatt didn't blame him. Exchange the street for desk work? No, thank you. The police department had tried it. Then it was bye-bye PD, hello marshals.

Jonah's mouth twitched, and Wyatt realized he'd been

staring at Nina, who had sat beside Sienna. His boss said, "Let's wait for Parker."

Parker walked in on his phone. "Okay, thanks. Bye."

He sat beside his wife and took a gulp of the coffee she'd set there. "Portland PD are in agreement that security should be stepped up even more on Theresa and Emily, and they've stationed officers outside Ronnie's hospital room. But they've got their hands full prepping for Monday's presidential visit to their fair city. I suggested protective custody with the marshals, and they jumped right on that."

Jonah nodded.

"Eric and Hailey are on their way to fetch Theresa and Emily now. They'll be back with them both by tonight, before which we'll have the safe house on O'Mara ready."

Nina sat back, a look of relief on her face. Wyatt knew how she felt. He wanted nothing to happen to Emily or Theresa if they could prevent it. Neither of them could live with that outcome. Too much had happened already, and Mr. Thomas had gotten too close to Emily as it was, even only by association. He'd met her, spied on her. Used her to distract them. And neither Wyatt nor Nina wanted him to turn his attention to Emily the way he had with them. Or the way he had with Ronnie.

He sighed. Jonah looked as if he wanted to say something, but what was there to be said? They'd lost people before. It never felt good even when they'd only come close to it.

"I'm glad they'll be safe." Nina's voice was small.

Wyatt gave her what was supposed to be a reassuring look. "As much as we can make sure of it, they will be."

She nodded, but there was no visible change in her demeanor. Maybe later they should try that hug again, see if the effects could last longer. It had been seriously the best hug he'd gotten in his entire life. This whole thing was uncharted territory for him. But at least it had made him forget about how badly his throat hurt.

Parker spoke. "We also spoke to Emily's father. He's heading home today."

"You got a hold of him?" Wyatt figured Parker's navy SEAL background gave him some pull in the military community.

But Parker said, "Not me. Sienna."

Sienna smiled. "It was easier than I thought."

Wyatt shook his head. He'd never met anyone so disinclined to give up their angle. Nina was the same way, and it drove him nuts at the same time he wanted to spend more and more time with Nina just so he could keep peeling back layers as she opened up to him.

Her mother's and father's tragedies were big, but he wanted to know the small things as well. The regular stuff. The stuff no one really thought was all that important, but when it was taken away felt like everything. He never wanted to get to that place with Nina—the place where he started to take her for granted. Their relationship would likely not go anywhere long-term; they were too different. It was why he was holding back. But he couldn't deny there was something about her that drew him.

It was a possibility.

A whole lot of hope, and not much else besides. But he'd never felt that before, not for anyone.

"Want to walk us through what Mr. Thomas said to you?"

Wyatt glanced at his boss. He didn't especially want to rehash any of it, and definitely not in front of Nina. But he told them anyway about what Mr. Thomas had said of Wyatt and his father. Wyatt had figured he would tell Nina about his move to the marshals at some point. Apparently that was going to be now.

"I guess he thought, like all those other people in the department, that my father had compromised the investigation somehow. Mostly because they didn't want to believe what had happened."

Jonah and Parker knew the details, so he turned to Nina. "It was a murder case. A six-year-old girl... It was grisly, let's just leave it at that. He worked it for months, pounding pavement, knocking on doors. He wasn't eating, wasn't sleeping. He had a heart attack, and he went right back to work. Didn't slow down. My mom threatened to divorce him just to get through to him. She moved in with her sister, and he kept at it. Whatever was in him that wouldn't let go, it had my dad in a choke hold. He would not quit."

Wyatt knew what it was, because the same thing was inside him.

Nina said, "Did he find the killer?"

Wyatt swallowed. "He was running on fumes, pulling out all the stops to find this guy. By the time they figured out who he was, they tore over to his place with an arrest warrant, but it was too late. There was another missing girl. They found the guy with her body. She'd been dead half an hour.

"Everyone figured he messed up somewhere, that he missed a step on the evidence and that was why this little girl had died. They knew how torn up he was feeling because they felt the same way. But they twisted it, assuming it really was his fault because they needed someone to blame. They didn't want to believe that there would be a day for all of them when they wouldn't be able to save someone."

"And you transferred out of that department to the marshals."

"They all thought he must have either shared the details of the case with me, and I missed it, too. Which means I shouldn't be doing the job. Or I should have stopped him, convinced him somehow to hand off the case. Then the little girl wouldn't have died."

His voice was sardonic, angry. It grated his own ears, but he'd kept all this bottled up for so long it was spilling out now and he couldn't stop it. "Any sequence of events that meant she didn't die, they'd have been fine with. Anything other than what actually happened."

"Wyatt—"

He shook his head. "I haven't talked about it up until now because I don't want to rehash it. You can't fix it, because there's nothing to fix."

Jonah's phone beeped at the same time as both Parker's and Wyatt's.

Jonah's gaze was on his screen. "Conference call time."

He connected the call.

Sienna reached out for Nina's hand and held it firmly in hers. Nina would much rather it was Wyatt holding her hand, but apparently that wasn't going to happen anytime soon. Not that she blamed him.

Wyatt's story about his father had been so sad. Caught up in the investigation of a child's murder, unable to rest? No wonder his father had been so distraught when another child had died that he'd quit. Nina almost wondered if Wyatt wouldn't have done exactly the same thing. Not out of stubbornness, but strength. He was so unyielding, and perhaps he'd seen so much of himself in his father's actions, or saw himself heading in the same direction and had pulled away from police work.

Maybe she was only grasping at straws. He'd said he had a case of his own at that time, but she'd gotten to know him over the last three days. She'd seen his heart, the way it had softened to Emily and Theresa. The way he'd been torn up after Tashi was shot. A child's murder would have rocked him the way it had rocked his father.

Jonah introduced them all, and through the phone's speaker the cop replied, "Nice to meet ya, fellas." The man had a gravelly voice. "Wyatt."

Wyatt shifted in his chair in a way Nina didn't think he'd have done if the detective could see him. "Mike." He glanced at them. "Mike was my father's partner."

"Before he quit to go golf every day while I get to train a child to be a police officer."

Wyatt chuckled low in his throat. "Rookie?"

"He has pimples."

Wyatt laughed aloud. "What do you have on the Ronnie Walters case so far?"

Mike's voice changed from jovial to serious like a switch had been flipped. "One shot to the chest. Left in bed. No lights on. Door was locked behind him when he left her there. Kids were both sleeping over with friends. She's in intensive care, fighting for her life."

Nina's head spun, processing it all. "So he tried to kill Wyatt because I involved him in this, and then he drove back to Portland in time to try to kill Ronnie while her whole family was conveniently not home?"

"He had to have known," Mike said. "Surveilled her enough to know she would have been alone last night. We got a partial fingerprint that we're running. He messed up, and now we're going to get him."

Nina frowned. In one night he'd left a fingerprint at Ronnie's and DNA with Wyatt? *Sloppy* wasn't a word she would use to describe Mr. Thomas, not in the least. And yet it was happening again and again. He didn't strike her as ever doing anything that wasn't 100 percent intentional. It just wasn't possible that he'd been sloppy twice, not when it might lead them to find out who he was when they tested both.

Unless that was his intention.

Mr. Thomas might know—or want—things to come to a head, and for this to be over. Perhaps he was setting that up on purpose, to be free of what he'd done and move on. To end Nina's investigation. Which meant he was likely making plans to kill her and tie up every loose end in the process.

Wyatt's eyes were on her when he said, "Caliber?"

Mike answered. "Forty-five."

Parker whistled. "Overkill."

"Mighta been the only gun he could get a hold of on short notice," Mike said. "Or, yeah, he was making a statement. Either fits. We're running ballistics to see if we can get a match."

Nina's foot tapped the floor as she processed the information against what she knew about pathology. There were reasons for every action. No one ever did anything without meaning to, either consciously or unconsciously.

Wyatt said, "He's keeping to his MO even while he's off the plan."

"Cleaning up all the loose ends."

He nodded. Nina was glad he was tracking with her, even though she didn't want to talk about the fact that she'd inadvertently made Wyatt a target. It made her feel better that someone else understood what they were up against. Mr. Thomas had switched from attempted kidnapping and intimidation to attempted murder.

As far as they knew, he hadn't killed since Emily's mother.

"Or trying," she said.

All they needed was enough evidence to prove it was him beyond reasonable doubt in a courtroom. And yes, Nina had every intention of being the one who helped the police get that. She wanted nothing less than for Mr. Thomas to be in prison for the remainder of his natural life. That, and a pardon for her father. Justice for her mother.

Then Nina would be free of him.

Mike spoke. "I'll work my end. Work your end and we'll pool resources. We'll nail this guy sooner or later." He bit out the words, and Nina wondered if he didn't think of his partner, Wyatt's father, and the little girl's death. Maybe Mike had to force himself not to rush through every case, just in case someone else's life was at stake. A case like that had to have affected him, even if it wasn't in the way it had affected Wyatt's dad. It had to be a thought that crossed his mind with every investigation. She knew it would cross hers.

Nina was feeling the bite of the clock at her heels. Time was running out for them, as it had already almost done for Ronnie.

She couldn't think about the woman, or Nina would be overwhelmed with guilt over her being hurt. Mr. Thomas's actions were his doing, even though it felt like they should have been able to prevent this. That maybe they'd be able to end the cycle of his terror and violence before anyone else suffered. *God, I'm so sorry Ronnie is hurt.* She squeezed her eyes shut. *Please don't let anyone else get hurt before we figure out who Mr. Thomas really is, and he gets arrested. I don't want anyone else to suffer.*

Sienna squeezed her hand. Nina squeezed back and let go as she lifted her head.

"In the meantime," Mike said. "You wanna tell me how he got the drop on you, Wyatt?"

Wyatt's lips twitched. "He's bigger?"

Mike barked out a laugh. "You didn't call for help, you just lay there? What's wrong with you, boy?"

"Mike." Wyatt said his name like it was a warning. "Parker found a blocking device outside my house that jammed all cell service. There was nothing I could do. Thomas planned this. He made sure I'd be cut off from everyone who could help. Still, I winged him in Karl's backyard, and I used that to my advantage. It's why he couldn't kill me before I got to my backup weapon."

"You gotta be smart, boy. I don't wanna be calling up your daddy to tell him you expired next time because some nutcase outthought you."

"I know."

"You better call him. He knows you were in town. He's been trying to get a hold of you."

Wyatt's cheek moved like he'd bitten it on the inside. "Did you catch this case, or just volunteer to fill us in so you could harass me about this?"

"No comment."

"Mike. Seriously?"

"I had gallbladder surgery three weeks ago. I'm on a desk pushing paper, didn't even go to the scene on this. Come on, Wyatt. Give an old man the chance to do something remotely interesting. I'm dying of boredom over here." Mike barked his laugh again. "Golfing with your dad is looking exciting at this point."

"I'm sure it is." Wyatt leaned forward to end the call. "Goodbye, Mike."

"Don't you dare—"

Wyatt hung up on him and sat back, muttering something about a "meddling old man."

"I'm sure he means well," Nina offered.

"He needs to mind his own business."

He was shutting her out. Nina could see it in his face. He'd shared with them what was going on, and about his past, but he'd evidently reached his limit. Did he think she wasn't prepared to be part of whatever was going on with him? She was happy to support him, but apparently he didn't want that from her. He wanted to help her, but he wasn't willing to accept the same back.

From the looks of it, while he was determined to protect himself from whatever was between him and his father, it was having the opposite effect.

Jonah opened his mouth to address them all, but the door swung open. A slight man in a baggy suit stuck his head in. "Results came back on your DNA. The lab is *not* happy about how many phone calls they got asking for it to be rushed. I think they did the test just to get you all off their backs."

Wyatt sat up. "And?"

"No match. He's not in any database anywhere, and his picture isn't anywhere online that the computer could find. They ran them *all*." The man's expression sank. "It's the computer age—who isn't online? I don't know who this guy is y'all are looking for, but he basically doesn't exist."

ELEVEN

Wyatt tapped the end of his cheap pen on the desk. How were they supposed to find a guy who didn't exist? Everyone had their picture online these days. Not to mention they also had DNA and a partial fingerprint from Mr. Thomas. Those could help, but Wyatt hesitated to believe they would.

He gripped the desk phone to his ear. "That's everything we have."

"Okay," Wyatt's cousin Geoff said. "That's great. There's never been evidence before, not in any of the cases listed as possibly linked. When I fill in the special agent assigned, he'll probably be ecstatic to hear that Mr. Thomas slipped up."

"Nina doesn't think so." Wyatt glanced at her, sitting at the spare desk across from him and doing something with her phone. "She thinks he left evidence on purpose."

"And you?"

"I'm inclined to agree, but we don't know for sure. We still have to run it, because if he does want to get caught, or however he thinks this will end, it's the job. He needs to be brought to justice."

Geoff said, "I'll contact the special agent assigned to

that case and let him know. I still didn't hear back from my email two days ago, so if I don't hear anything by end of day I'll call you back."

"All right. Let me know."

"Be careful."

Wyatt caught Nina's gaze and said, "I will." He hung up and told Nina what Geoff had said.

"You mean that he's going to come back and end *you* on purpose."

Wyatt didn't regret telling her it was likely Mr. Thomas intended to return and finish him off. "He tried to kill me, and then Ronnie. Of course he's going to come back and try again. He's probably seriously mad right now."

Her mouth dropped open, her eyes wide. "And I'm not allowed to be concerned about that?"

"About me?"

"Of course! Who else? This is basically my fault. He knows I told you, so he's coming after you."

People in the office were starting to stare. Wyatt didn't blame them, if the drama playing out between him and Nina was more interesting than paperwork. But he had to know, and she had to say it. Out loud. Because Mr. Thomas had seen something in Nina in Tashi's backyard when she'd yelled his name that had made him turn his attention to Wyatt, and he needed to know why he'd thought there was a connection between them.

She made a frustrated sound deep in her throat that was more amusing than anything else. Plus cute. He let his gaze move over her face. Definitely cute. She said, "I'm not supposed to care about you?"

"I am a very care-about-able person."

"That made no sense." But she smiled, and wasn't that the whole point?

"Do you want me to feel bad that he's more concerned with me than you right now? I don't want him anywhere near you, Nina. I'd rather you packed your bags and disappeared to a desert island to lie on the beach while I go out and catch this guy."

She sighed. "We've already had this conversation. I've spent most of my adult life in countries where I didn't speak the language beyond a couple of phrases that involved 'infiltrate' or 'semiautomatic.' I'd like to stay in America if that's okay with you."

He shrugged, feeling the pull of a smile on his lips. "Hawaii works for me."

And why was he now picturing her on a beach, walking *with him*, smiling? Wearing his ring. No, no, no. That wasn't the plan. Marriage? Wyatt had never been that type, even if Nina had that sweet PTA-mom look about her while still knowing how to kill a man twice her size with her thumb. It was kind of irresistible. But he would resist.

"I don't want him to hurt you." Her words were soft.

"Ditto."

She broke out of whatever had been subduing her and chuckled. "So noted." She sighed. "I guess we're at an impasse, then."

"Or you watch my back, and I watch yours."

"That could work." She tipped her head to the side. "Did Geoff say anything else of note?"

"He's going to put in the request to run the photo and the partial print through the databases he has access to while he's waiting for the other agent to get back to him. And he's going to ask them to run everything through Interpol's database, since we didn't get anything out of our test or on the photo."

"You think he's some kind of international criminal?"

Wyatt shrugged. "We know he's never been in the military, and he's never been convicted of a crime either, otherwise we'd have his name. Who knows? Maybe Geoff's search will turn up something and the FBI will be able to put together enough evidence to get a takedown for all the murders, not just Ronnie's injury and Tashi's shooting."

Nina nodded slowly, quiet again. "That would be nice."

"Dinner would be nice. An arrest warrant is relative, in the grand scheme of things."

"The grand scheme being your stomach?"

Wyatt shrugged. "I am hungry. And we've been sitting here all day."

Nina sat alone at the restaurant table. She didn't want to look around that office again. They'd all started giving her that weird "she's freaking out" face *again*. She was done being the one everyone knew about and felt sorry for. At least Wyatt seemed to get it. He cared about her, or so she thought. Maybe as much as she cared about him.

It was strange to know she had the attention of a good man. Nina figured she could certainly get used to it, especially when it was the first time in her life it had happened. She hadn't spent much time with a good man, not this much time, really ever. They had been thrown together through some insane circumstances, but she was determined that Mr. Thomas's actions weren't going to ruin any of it.

Something was happening between her and Wyatt. Something Nina thought might be huge—caring, affection. Attraction. All of it was there in spades, and she prayed it wouldn't get crushed. The thin strands that

seemed to stretch between them were like the most deli-
cate of silk thread, so beautiful but so fragile. Anything
could snap them, and then it would all be severed and
there would be nothing but what could have been.

Nina flipped her phone, end over end, on top of the
table. She'd finished her soda twenty minutes ago and
hadn't started on the refill the waitress had brought that
she didn't want. Who needed that much caffeine?

She dropped the phone to thumb through her texts, not
really expecting anything new. But there it was. *Baltimore Public Library.* Nina wasn't the type to sit back and
do nothing. Especially after years of covert operations.

Nina bit her lip, not thinking about it overly much,
and typed.

Who are you?

It wasn't that she expected a reply, but she had to do
something. Hanging around like a sitting duck hadn't
ever been her forte. Ask Sienna. And so maybe it had gotten her in trouble when Sienna had amnesia and Nina had
dropped off the CIA's radar to stick by her and make sure
she wasn't in trouble. But it wasn't every day when international criminals crawled out of the woodwork wanting
her best friend dead or alive.

Wyatt wound through the tables headed in her direction. He looked so strong, so capable of carrying all this
on his shoulders. Nina knew from experience that old
adage was true—the bigger he was, the harder he would
fall when Mr. Thomas decided to finish him off for good.

Nina wasn't going to let that happen.

Her phone buzzed on the tabletop. She swiped to see
the text reply.

That is the question.

"Something good?"

She glanced up at Wyatt, and the phone dropped from her hand to clatter on the table.

"Guilty face." He smirked. "Are you sure you were a spy?"

"Rusty spy." She got up, swiped up her phone and purse, and headed out of the restaurant ahead of him. The cat-and-mouse game Mr. Thomas was intent on playing was getting to her. She knew that. Her stomach burned, and it wasn't the sandwich she'd just eaten.

Nina halted halfway to the car, so fast Wyatt nearly slammed into her back. "You know what? Forget this." Nina pulled up the contact and dialed the number.

"Little Mouse." His voice was smooth, but with an edge to it that made her want to throw up thinking about those shots he'd put in Tashi.

"Who are you?"

Wyatt's whole body jerked. He moved as though he wanted to grab the phone and smash the thing on the asphalt of the parking lot. Nina stepped back, determined to make Mr. Thomas reveal too much or mess up somehow. "I asked you a question."

"My, my."

Wyatt turned away; he got on his phone, talking about "traces" and "locations." At least he wasn't glaring at her anymore.

"Tell me. I want to know. I should know. Why do you think it's been *years*, and I won't give this up? You killed my mother, and my father is dead because of you. Now you try to kill Ronnie. Sorry that didn't work out."

"That was her name?"

Like he didn't know. "I'm going to figure out who you are."

"Perhaps. It has been years, and you haven't managed it yet, Little Mouse."

Nina gritted her teeth. "In the meantime if I hear you touched Emily or got anywhere near her, or even looked in her direction, I will bring my entire arsenal down on your head."

He chuckled.

When it didn't cease, Nina spoke over it. "I promise you."

She hung up. He wasn't going to give her anything. That was a stupid thing, and she shouldn't have done it, but she was just so *mad*.

"You shouldn't have done that." She turned to Wyatt. "You hung up before we could get a location." He lifted his hands and let them fall back to his sides. "Do you at least feel better? Because it didn't help in any other way."

She glared at him.

"Nina?"

Mr. Thomas had killed her mother. He'd sentenced her father to incarceration and death behind bars. And Wyatt thought she was trying to *feel better*?

He took a step toward her.

Nina took a step back.

"Ni—"

She lifted one hand, palm out. "Don't come near me." Her cheeks were hot, almost tickling.

"Honey, you're crying."

Nina blinked. She swiped at her cheeks, and her fingers came away wet. "I—" She choked on the word. Her breath came in gasps. Nina bent forward and hung her head, trying to stop the spinning in her mind. She couldn't think. She could barely get air. Her throat was blocked. Tears streamed down her face, and she realized she was crying aloud.

Wyatt lifted her up so she was standing. But she didn't have the strength. He held her weight while she cried for her mother, for her father. Had she ever actually done that before?

She wasn't sure she had.

Wyatt's hand rubbed up and down her back, and she clung to him, her body purging itself of all the pent-up emotion she'd been collecting for years. All of it surged to the surface. All the grief, all the fear. All the pain she'd never told anyone about, not even Sienna, really.

No one.

Wyatt settled in the armchair and watched Nina sleep. Curled up on his couch, she was covered in the afghan his mother had sent him last Christmas, taking a nap.

He had his own phone in his hand now. He didn't want Nina's cathartic crying to affect him, but it had. He couldn't deny the fact that seeing her expunge that much emotion made him wonder how he'd feel if something happened to his parents. To his father.

Through the entire investigation Wyatt had watched his dad, a man he'd idolized his whole life as the epitome of a strong, capable cop, just…diminish. He hadn't believed it at first, not willing to accept that anything could bring the old man down. But it had, and now Wyatt had seen it again, in Nina. He couldn't deny that even the strongest person could be brought low if the circumstances were bad enough.

Wyatt picked up the phone, and for the first time in months he dialed his father's number.

"Somebody kick it?"

Wyatt blinked at his father's fast response. "Nobody's dead." His dad thought a family emergency was the only reason he'd be calling. "Not that there haven't been a few near misses."

"Yeah, I heard about that. Serial killer, right?"

Wyatt reiterated everything again, not surprised at all that his dad had heard through the cop grapevine even given that he was retired. "I got Geoff on it."

"Good call," his dad said. "You really have no idea who he is?"

"Not yet."

"Okay."

His dad sounded like he was thinking through the problem. Assistance, coupled with the lack of extreme awkwardness that had been between them before, washed through him. Evidently they could be civil to each other when it was about police work, and likely not for any other reason. If necessary, Wyatt could spend the rest of his life with his relationship with his father being nothing but a cop-to-cop bond. He didn't want to do it, but he could.

"Dad?"

"Uh-oh, what?"

"You don't have to be like that." Wyatt sighed. "This doesn't have to be like that."

"What do you think it's going to be like? I quit my job. I couldn't handle it."

"You retired from the force."

"Because after thirty years of dealing with it, I finally caught a case that chewed me up and spit me out. So I decided to be done. I quit, and you transferred because you couldn't handle the fact that your old man couldn't hack the job. You didn't want to be around all the boys and gals, wondering if they thought you wouldn't be able to hack it either."

"That's not what it was."

Nina shifted in her sleep, so he got up and paced to his kitchen so as not to wake her.

"If you say so."

"I like being a marshal. I—"

"If you say so."

Wyatt glanced at the ceiling. "Will you let me finish? This isn't about me proving I've moved on or that I'm doing better. You retired. Apparently, you're fine with it. You caught the worst of cases, the one everyone dreads. Something awful happened. But do you know what I realized? I am like you. I've always been like you. And it hit me, because I'm so like you that I would have done the same thing. I did, faced with a case where the outcome didn't sit right with me. So I transferred."

"You wouldn't have let that little girl die." His dad's voice was gruff. "You wouldn't have messed up like I did."

"I like that you think that, even while I don't like it at the same time because I know it's not true."

"That makes no sense, Wy." His dad chuckled.

"It's not funny either."

"Seems funny to me," his dad said. "Funny a pair of cops can't see what's right in front of their faces."

Wyatt glanced back at the couch. Was there something right in front of his face now? He remembered how it had felt to take care of Nina when she was so upset, that it had made him hurt just to see and hear it.

"Anyhow, your mom wants you at lunch on Sunday."

"I'm in the middle of something."

"Know that. I stopped by to see Tashi at the hospital today. Bring the girl with you."

"Dad—"

"Nina, right?"

Wyatt glanced at the ceiling again. He really needed to clean up there. "I'll call Mom. We'll be there *if* we can make it. Things are pretty intense right now."

"I got that. I've been looking into it. I'll let you know if I connect anything."

"Thanks, Dad." And he really meant it. Another set of trained eyes—the eyes of a homicide detective—might help a great deal. They said goodbye, and Wyatt hung up.

He blew out a breath and went back to Nina. Things might actually be looking up finally. Mr. Thomas was out there, plotting who knew what. But in here, it was him and Nina, and whatever came next, she wasn't going to face it alone. Wyatt was going to make sure that they faced it together.

Nina rolled over on the couch and opened her eyes. "What happened now?"

Wyatt only smiled. But before he could answer her question, his tablet started to ring with an incoming video call.

TWELVE

He settled beside her on the couch and swiped to answer the call. "Hey, Geoff."

This must be Wyatt's cousin that he'd told her about. The FBI agent. The frown on the man's face was the first thing to register. His features bore a similarity to Wyatt, though Geoff was considerably more clean-cut. His gaze flickered to the side, her side, and he cracked a smile. "Nina Holmes?"

She nodded. "Hi."

Wyatt introduced her to his cousin, then said, "What's up?"

The frown came back. Whatever it was, Nina didn't think it was good. But then nothing had been good so far through this whole thing. Perhaps God would grant them something positive, finally, so that they might be able to stay strong through to the end. They needed an extra measure of grace in this. Nina had seen far too much of Mr. Thomas at work to believe he wasn't going to go down without a serious fight—whether he intended to allow himself to be caught or not.

Give us strength.

She'd asked Wyatt what he thought about the faith

Sienna and Parker had while they'd been driving. It had been a good conversation, where he'd told her he could see how it benefited their relationship to be on the same team—to have a mutual faith. But that didn't mean he'd experienced belief for himself. She wanted it for him, it was true. But there was no way Wyatt, being the man that he was, would ever believe because she pushed him. He was the kind of man who would have to wrestle within himself and come to a place of faith on his own.

Wyatt glanced at her with a question in his eyes, but she shook her head.

"I found something, if you guys are done making moony faces at each other. At least long enough to hear what I have to say."

Wyatt shot his cousin a look that told Nina exactly what he thought. "Go ahead."

Nina didn't react. He didn't need to know she hadn't expected his reaction to be so vehement. Wyatt apparently wasn't a fan—at all—of his cousin's commenting on how they were with each other. If they got into a relationship, was he going to hold back when other people could see? Why did it matter what people thought? It would only be a relationship between the two of them.

It was possible that years of solitude and secrets had affected her. Whereas Wyatt was someone who was more comfortable surrounded by other people. It was a big difference in their personalities, and likely something they were going to have to work to get over.

Nina realized she was making a lot of assumptions about where this was going. The reality of the situation was, Wyatt had become a big deal to her over the last few days. More than anyone else—aside from Sienna—

he had stood with her, willing to fight on her side, taking only her word that it was right.

Now that she had experienced it, Nina had no intention of giving it up.

"I took a look at the physical evidence you collected, the DNA results from under your fingernails that the crime lab forwarded. I ran it through our database at the Bureau and got a hit."

Nina shot upright. "You did?"

"Well, not a hit exactly. I still don't know who he is, but I came across something interesting I knew you'd want to know." Geoff took a breath, evidently as anxious to tell them as they were to hear it.

Wyatt sat upright as well. He set the tablet on the table so Geoff would be able to see them. Below the screen he reached out and grabbed her fingers. Apparently he still intended to support her, despite his reaction. That was something. But if the man couldn't show support even when his cousin teased him about it, well…it didn't bode well as far as Nina could see.

"Linked to the file I have on that identity, which is basically still no more than the police have except for this one thing—"

Wyatt cut in. "Will you speak English?"

"It doesn't go anywhere. There's only a firewall that doesn't let the user any further without the correct security clearance. It's—"

"Classified."

Wyatt jerked and looked at her. Nina broke her fingers from his hold and backed up on the couch as though Mr. Thomas were in the room and she needed to retreat. Immediately.

He stared at her. "Classified?"

"For a long time I thought he could've been a spy. There has to have been a reason why I'd think that. If he's tied up in the government somehow…it kind of makes sense. The stories he told." Nina worked her mouth to one side, then the other, as she processed. "Can you get access?"

Geoff shook his head. "I don't have the clearance. Neither does my boss. How about you?"

"She's retired."

Nina glanced at Wyatt. He wasn't wrong, given that she'd severed that tie since her retirement. Would the CIA want her calling them up for a favor?

Now that she knew for sure they might be able to tell her something, she would do it. Whether they minded or not. If someone she knew had the clout to get into this file, she would do everything she could to get that access.

People's lives depended on it.

"I can make a couple of calls."

Geoff nodded. "I'll send Wyatt what I have."

"Thank you." She snapped up her phone, not willing to waste even a minute. First, she called Sienna and filled her in. Then she left three voice mails, one only a series of numbers. Some things called for official channels, others decidedly unofficial ones. Nina wasn't taking chances—she was using both this time. Calling in all her favors.

She turned to find Wyatt standing in front of her.

"That's it?"

Nina shrugged. "There's a procedure. I have to wait for a callback now."

"You still have friends in the agency, even though you and Sienna both quit?"

"We were there a lot of years. Our handler might have

been sent to prison for betraying her country, but there were other people we worked with."

"Office Christmas parties?"

She couldn't help it; the smile slipped out. "You don't want to know what spies do for fun."

Wyatt chuckled. "No, I don't suppose I do." His face sobered. "Was it hard?"

"Going to strange places for so long that coming home felt like it was a foreign country. Spending time with men and women so evil they shouldn't have been allowed to live, but knowing mission parameters meant I couldn't kill them. Having barely any relationships because who could I trust?" Nina held his gaze. He had to know. "It was a soulless existence. But it was me, for a lot of years."

He stepped closer. "And now?"

"It's not something easily walked away from. That kind of life permeates everything. But living in this town, even chasing after Mr. Thomas, it's like seeing the sun for the first time after a storm that has lasted for years."

Wyatt touched her cheek. "I'm glad."

He inched in so slowly she didn't realize what he was doing at first. When his lips touched hers, Nina jumped, startled. He was warm. Strong. He had heart like she'd never seen in anyone before. Wyatt's sweater was soft under her fingers, the muscles of his forearms unrelenting. As they shared a sweet moment in the midst of everything happening, Nina leaned in, absorbing what it felt like to be cared for by a man she respected everything about—even the things others might see as weakness.

When he leaned back, she thought for a moment he might apologize. *Don't say sorry.* He cleared his throat and actually blushed. Had she ever done that in her life? "Okay. Right."

"Wyatt—"

"I have to call Parker, fill him in."

"I already told Sienna."

"Okay. Still…" He motioned over his shoulder.

Nina nodded. What else was she supposed to do? He'd kissed her, and now he was running away. He left the room, and Nina stared at the space where he'd been standing.

Frantic knocks on the front door were followed by the doorbell. Then more frantic knocking.

Wyatt called out, "I'll get it."

Wyatt stopped behind the closed door, gun ready. "Who is it?"

Parker answered, "Me and Sienna."

They had a code between them that meant "I'm under duress" but that wasn't it, so Wyatt opened the door. It was Sienna who pushed in the house first, carrying a giant bulky laptop with her that she lugged into the living room. "I found something. After I listened to your message I thought of something."

He and Parker followed, finding Sienna on the couch beside Nina.

As Wyatt sat on the coffee table in front of them, knees to knees, Nina scrubbed her hands down her face. She glanced at him, and they shared a smile, though hers was tentative.

He'd done that. The sting of it hit him like the cut of a knife, deep in his chest. She'd pulled back, now wary with him where before her trust had been evident. Wyatt's fear had distilled into guilt that he'd distracted her when she needed to focus. Had that kiss not been the right move?

Was he going to question everything now? His con-

versation with his father had put a lot of his concerns
to rest, but evidently not all. He should trust Nina the
way she had trusted him this entire time. Was it himself
that he didn't trust? His heart warred against his head,
knowing he could put his faith in her and she wouldn't
let him down.

So why had he given in and then pulled away?

"Tell them," Parker said to his wife.

"I'm finding the email." Sienna glanced at Nina.
"After you called me I hit up an old friend. Her name is
Sabine MacArthur. She was with the CIA, but it's sort
of complicated and we don't have time for a long story.
She got in touch with her contacts, some still in the CIA,
and we got to the bottom of this classified file. It seriously took like half an hour. She's *that* good." She clicked
twice and then bent the laptop back on itself to make it
look like a tablet. She read aloud from memory what was
there. "His name is Steve Adams."

Nina gasped. Wyatt's gaze flicked over to her, then
back to Sienna. "What?"

Sienna said, "And he's dead."

Wyatt didn't move. "Explain."

Sienna shifted to face Nina. "Steve Adams was a career CIA agent. Commendations, awards. You name it,
he's received one for his outstanding work in the field of
espionage." She clicked the screen, showing a file photo
of Mr. Thomas.

Nina nodded.

"A while back Sabine and her husband had some trouble. Steve Adams was her contact at the CIA, and he was
reported to have been killed during that time. His body
was, in fact, delivered to the CIA along with a bomb that
destroyed all the evidence. There was enough to confirm

that a male of his size had been killed, and given that they were told it was Steve Adams and that he never surfaced after that, the case was closed."

"So he faked his own death?" Wyatt didn't like this, not one bit.

Sienna nodded. Nina was completely pale. If he reached out to hold her hand, would she accept his touch? It was more likely she would reject him, and Wyatt didn't know if he could handle that in front of their friends. Option B was that Nina would let him do it, but not because she wanted to. She might allow him to hold her hand because she didn't want to make a scene about not wanting to. Which would be a whole lot worse.

So he kept his hand to himself.

Sienna continued, "Somehow he made whoever tried to kill him and plant that bomb with his body think he was dead. Or he was in collusion with that person and got their help to disappear…we don't know. Sabine couldn't believe it when I told her that this guy, Mr. Thomas, was still alive and coming after you. She was very concerned.

"The only thing that stopped her from hopping on a plane and coming here to help is the fact that her first baby is due in three weeks." Sienna smiled. "Her husband called me five minutes after. Wanted to know everything about this. He's coming home from whatever job he was out on, and he'll protect Sabine. He doesn't want her anywhere near this."

Parker shifted. "Of course not."

Wyatt nodded.

Nina and Sienna shared a smile, and Nina said, "You guys would say that. And the only reason I agree with you is because she's pregnant."

Sienna nodded. "So two minutes after I hung up with

Doug, Sabine called me back. She'd done more research, and found Steve Adams's old handler. The man who oversaw his career for years."

Nina gasped. "You know who it is?"

Sienna nodded. "He's an old man now, retired for a long time. He lives in Montana at a ranch with his granddaughter and her husband."

"Let's go."

Wyatt held up his hand to Nina. "Hold up a second. If this man was Mr. Thomas's, or Steve Adams's, or whatever we're calling him now's handler, how do we know he's not aware of all of this? He has to know something is wrong with the man, maybe not everything. The kills were spaced well apart, far enough he could have been off the radar, maybe on personal time. But while it might not be all that hard to hide a sickness like this from people who don't know you that well, or don't see you that often, I get the feeling you guys are pretty close with your handlers."

Sienna nodded. "We are."

"That's why we have to talk to him," Nina said. "We need to know what he knows so we can catch Mr. Thomas. The handler will know his quirks, his weaknesses. We'll have a shot at getting him to slip up. He's had the advantage this whole time, and we've been scrambling to get ahead of him. Now we can. For the first time we might have enough information that we can figure out his next move before he makes it."

THIRTEEN

Just after dawn the next morning they disembarked from a small and alarmingly rickety plane on the runway of a Montana ranch. Wyatt led the way while Nina walked behind him. He'd been pretty quiet, probably tired compounding on top of tired, she figured. Nina glanced back at Parker, still in the plane, and he gave her a thumbs-up.

Nina turned back to the ranch, where cement walkways crossed the land between them and the barn and house. It looked like that kids' game where the players climbed ladders and slid down chutes. The front porch stretched to the right front corner of the house, ending a ramp from which emerged a barrel-chested man in a wheelchair with a shotgun laid across his lap.

Wyatt grasped her elbow to halt her progress. She frowned at him, not in the least bit threatened by the man now wheeling toward them. Had Wyatt asked, she wouldn't have been able to tell him why she didn't feel the man meant them any harm. She just didn't.

Nina said, "Abe Turnel?"

"Depends who's asking." His gruff voice made Nina think of her father during a golf tournament. *Hush up, girl. I'm trying to watch.* The memory formed a lump in her throat she had to fight past to speak again. Thankfully Wyatt introduced them both. The old man sighed. "You should come in."

They followed him up the ramp to the open yellow front door. The inside was clean, decorated with feminine touches like fresh flowers on the coffee table that matched the pillows on the couch.

A young woman stood in the kitchen at the stove, probably early twenties.

"Bridget."

She spun, a pleasant smile on her face. "Yeah, Pops?" She blinked at the two of them, stood in the doorway and then glanced at her grandfather. "You have company."

"Don't get too excited, kid. They'll be gone in an hour. It's a work thing."

Bridget eyed Nina, then Wyatt. "They're plumbers, too?"

No one moved. Thankfully, if they had to have some kind of cover story, Wyatt's badge wasn't on his belt.

Bridget grinned.

"Scram, kid."

"Whatever, Pops." Bridget narrowed her eyes at her grandfather's tone and then her lips twitched. "I'll be in the barn until Bill comes in for lunch. I have clay to fire."

Abe nodded. Before Bridget left, she poured coffee for each of them and plated three cinnamon rolls. Abe wheeled over to a spot at the table where there was no chair to pull out. Wyatt and Nina sat opposite him. If Nina had to guess, she'd say that Bridget was ecstatic her grandfather had company and it wasn't something that happened often, if at all. She would also guess that Bridget knew exactly who her grandfather had been before he retired.

The old man glanced at the closed door and reached for the sugar bowl. He spooned two heaps into his mug and stirred, a small smile of defiance on his face. "I always figured one day someone would show up out of the blue to see me." His voice was like sand being poured out.

Nina had to know if he was bound by some kind of confidentiality agreement, or whether he would be able to speak to them freely. "Is there any kind of gag order in place?"

The CIA could be a tricky animal, especially when a person retired. Just because she wasn't part of it anymore didn't mean she was free to speak of the things she'd seen and done while she worked there. She figured the same was true of Abe Turnel, though they were allowed to tell those closest to them who they were—after filling out a ream of paperwork to disclose the disclosure.

Abe's chest jerked, which Nina decided might have been laughter. "They could try." He sighed again. "But nah, not about this. They don't even know, and it's not in any official or unofficial report. Tried to tell them, but they never listened. Not once, not about him. Golden boy, everyone thought so. Reports I filed were misplaced or simply disappeared. He continued going on missions. Lauded for his work. Years had passed before I could no longer ignore what was happening. I made up my mind to confront him. Two weeks later I wake up in the hospital with a fractured back and a whole lot of healing wounds. So here I am, years gone by. I've been 'retired,' and Steve Adams is nowhere to be found."

Wyatt set his mug on the table. "What do you know about him faking his death?"

The old man snorted. "I hear things, even now. Wasn't surprised, but didn't believe for a second he was in that box when it blew up outside Langley." He made a *tut* sound with this tongue and shook his head.

"Since then, he's attempted to kill again." Nina gripped her cup to hide the fact her hand shook. "We need your help. He singled us out. I think he's trying to tie up all the loose ends. Everyone who might be able to point a finger at him for murder, any of the murders."

Abe pressed his lips together, then said, "How many?"

"Six," Wyatt said.

Abe shut his eyes.

"Anything you can tell us might help us to get ahead of him." Nina's stomach was clenched tight. "He killed my mother, and my father went to prison for it. The other day we met a young girl, Emily. He killed her mother, too. He tried to kill the mother's best friend because she talked to us. Another woman was shot in the leg. This is getting out of control. That's why we're here."

Abe opened his eyes, grief raw on his face. There was nothing about him that suggested what he had been—a career CIA handler. She knew the type, and it had all bled from him either because he'd been out of the business for so long, or because of what Steve Adams had done to him. All that was left was a broken-down old man who wanted to rest, but couldn't do that until the weight was lifted from his soul.

"I'm sorry to drag you into this. Especially if it puts you in harm's way. That isn't our intention."

"I'm already in it." The old man's eyes were wet. "I'm ready if he wants to come at me. He won't harm my family. They know as much as they can know, and they are both prepared."

Wyatt nodded. It was the same kind of solidarity she'd seen between Wyatt and Parker, who had stayed with the plane. A man-to-man, protect-those-we-love mentality that left her feeling cared for—in a slightly smothered way.

Nina had held her own, once when Mr. Thomas had drugged and then tried to abduct her from her apartment, and the other when he'd shot Kashi.

Steve Adams was a highly trained covert agent with years of experience. He was bigger, and stronger, than her, and yet he hadn't succeeded in his plan to take her somewhere and kill her. Not so far, at least. *Thank You, Lord.*

Nina said, "Is there anything you can tell us? Ideally we need to find him, but somehow I think we're going to have to lay out bait. It has to be strong enough to lure him out in a way that we're not caught off guard. We have to be prepared to take him down, but he has to walk into it not knowing what we're doing."

"You're talking about a twisted, sadistic man who is extremely adept at covert operations. I've never seen anything like it, not in all the years I was with the agency. The man was unparalleled. That's why the powers that be refused to believe he was a merciless killer. He was their star, and they poured time, money and all the resources they could find into cultivating his skills."

Nina nodded. She had known this wasn't going to be easy, but she'd been prepared for it. "He's slipping. I can't even really put my finger on it, but he's losing his grip. Wyatt shot at him, and he fled." She motioned to him, beside her. "Then he showed up at Wyatt's house and attempted to kill him. He's having to adjust his plan and adapt to what we're throwing at him. It's catching him off guard, but we need to step it up, otherwise we have no chance whatsoever of bringing him in. We may as well let him kill us all."

Abe stared at her with a combination of respect and a smidge of what she figured was him thinking she was insane. Not anything new. He pushed away his cinnamon roll and interlaced his fingers on the table. "I'm going to tell you a story. Do with it what you will, but maybe it will help you understand why this is essentially a fool's errand."

Wyatt had lost his appetite also. Anger burned in hot flames that filled his body and threatened to spill out. He could not believe the CIA had let a madman go unchecked for *years*, costing six people their lives. The arrogance was unbelievable, but then he figured that was par for the course with an agency that did everything under cover of darkness, cloaked in secrecy.

And Nina had worked for them.

She'd been part of that culture of lies, perpetrating who knew whose agenda in the world. As far as he was concerned, she could never have been completely certain that her orders came from the right people. If everything was done all cloak-and-dagger style, how had she made sure she wasn't perpetrating some crazy person's sick agenda?

Take Steve Adams, for example. The man had been celebrated, given authority over others. A certain degree of autonomy he had used for his own agenda. There was no way he hadn't been killing innocent women on the side and not brought that lack of morals and empathy into his workplace to watch people suffer the consequences.

And get away with it.

"It was nearly forty-five years ago now, and it was his

first mission." Abe sighed, as though simply saying it out loud was painful. "He was young, but tasked with getting close to a young Frenchwoman whose brother it was believed had ties to a group of Spanish separatists that don't even exist now. She had a four-year-old daughter.

"As the weeks passed he began to miss check-in. He would file a report that gave us nothing and say he needed more time. So I went to look in on the situation and found him playing house with her. Taking the little girl to school. When I was asked to apply pressure to my agent, to remind him he wasn't living in the real world and that he needed to finish the job, he responded. The information was delivered the next day, and the takedown of the Spaniards was effected."

Abe sighed. "But I'd seen something in him. Something about Steve Adams and that woman, her child... it was... I don't even know how to explain it other than to say it was *desperate*. So I looked into Steve's childhood. His father remarried when Steve was twelve, and the woman had a daughter. Something must have happened, something that sparked a sickness in Steve Adams that means he latches on to women with daughters. He develops a bond with them and when he kills the mother, the daughter is set free. That's what he said to me before he put me in this chair permanently. He thinks he's doing them a favor.

"The only thing I could see that might explain it would be that Steve's stepmom was hurting her daughter somehow, though there were never any reports. Steve's stepmother died of heart problems that could easily have been the result of a poison, but an autopsy was never done. His father died years after, but before I could talk to him. It's entirely possible that either Steve or his father killed the wife and Steve transfers that to each of his victims, whether the mother was hurting her child or not."

Beside him Nina gritted her teeth. "Mine never did."

"It's possible, that first mission, the target may have been hurting her daughter. But I could never find anything other than hearsay to back that up, though I talked to several people who knew her." Abe paused. "Something happened to Steve Adams, and we may never know what it was. All I have is theories and speculation. The likelihood that he'll explain himself one day isn't more than wishful thinking. But there is something wrong with him, something broken that no one will ever be able to fix."

Nina shut her eyes. Wyatt slid his hand under the ends of her hair to touch her neck. He gave her a gentle squeeze to impart some strength, or maybe give support if she needed it. His heart felt like it was tearing in two, for her. He didn't want her anywhere near a serial killer bent on making his last stand with Nina. Was it wrong that he would rather it was anyone else in the world than her? But she was determined not to allow any more collateral damage.

It was enough to make Wyatt want to pray for Emily, to double her protection and to make sure Steve Adams didn't get anywhere near her. Neither of them needed that on their consciences. There was no way they would walk away from it.

"It was the beginning of a pattern I saw repeat itself over and over. Missions he fell too deep into. People who were never the same after they met with him. It was bizarre, like some kind of mind-altering drug that he possessed with only his words. He left them reeling, like they'd been struck in the face and he'd never even touched them."

"What about the kills?" Wyatt asked. "Surely you had to have known he took lives where it was not part of the sanctioned mission."

Abe blew out a breath. "That first, the Frenchwoman? She was found dead weeks later. Steve had been on respite, between missions. He went off radar during the time she was killed. I searched and searched, but could never prove he went out of the country. Still, I had my suspicions. In all these years that's all I had. Never any proof, not until I confronted him. But I knew."

Nina shuddered under Wyatt's hand. "What can you tell us about his favorite places to go, or where he might go to ground?"

"He's a nomad. Homeschooled by a father who believed experiencing the world was an education in itself, so he was dragged all over. Europe, India, China, Australia. The US and Canada. It made him a better agent, understanding cultural differences the way he did, and his ability to blend in with locals. But he favored the US. Always came back here, I think because his parents considered it home. They had a place in Texas, but without the drawl. You'd never guess that's where he was from."

Wyatt tapped the table with his fingers, trying to think like the homicide detective part of him that he would always be. He'd never been as good as his father, but he'd certainly been heading that direction.

If anyone could figure out Steve Adams's next move, it was Nina. Who better to catch a spy than a spy? Wyatt only needed to convince her that it was possible for her to out-think Steve Adams. She'd known him, had thought about him, for years. It was primarily the memories of a traumatized child, but Steve Adams was clearly attached to her. Likely to each of the children of the mothers he'd killed—children he'd freed from whatever they had been subjected to. Or children he, in his twisted mind, had conceived they had been subjected to when in reality they were normal, healthy children.

"What happened to the Frenchwoman's daughter?"

The question emerged before Wyatt had even thought it through all the way, but it made sense. Maybe she would be able to help them bait Steve Adams.

Abe's head jerked. "I looked into her. She went to live with an aunt and now works at a Paris bank. There was no indication Steve Adams ever made further contact with her."

Wyatt stood and held out his hand. "Thank you. And thank you for your time."

Nina glanced at him but got up. She didn't want to leave. She looked like she had a whole lot more questions, but the lines around Abe Turnel's face had deepened. There was more going on medically with this man than simply old age and a spinal injury. He'd been attentive for long enough, but he was fading fast.

He wheeled his chair behind them to the door and sat on the porch as they walked down the steps.

Wyatt wanted to grab her hand and hold it. As much to reassure her as to feel her warmth and the beat of her pulse under his fingers. They were alive, and he was going to make sure they stayed that way.

Wyatt turned back to thank the man one more time before they went to the plane and headed home.

The red dot sat dead center on Abe Turnel's chest.

"Gun!"

Both Wyatt and Nina dived toward Abe as a shot rang

out. The wheelchair tipped back and they landed in a tangle of limbs. Wyatt felt Abe start to shake under them and looked up.

He was laughing. "Kids these days. They all want to be heroes."

Crack. The gunfire continued. Shot after shot with seconds' pause between each. Abe's fuzzy brow crinkled.

From the plane, Parker yelled, "No! Stay back!" Wyatt glanced up to see Bridget at the barn door.

"You get out of here." Abe frowned. "You get Steve Adams away from my granddaughter."

The next shot hit the wall just above Wyatt's head.

FOURTEEN

Nina flinched. Would the gunshots ever stop? A guttural sound emerged from her throat. She screamed at Wyatt, words she didn't even know she was saying. He ran to her and lifted her up, still yelling, and carried her with him while Abe Turnel yelled, "Go! Go!" from his prone position on the porch.

Shots slammed the house in a row closer and closer toward them. The boom reverberated across the valley. Was Steve Adams going to shoot the plane? They would never be able to get out of here then. How had he even found them?

Wyatt set her on her feet and raced across the grass, pulling her along after him, his head low as Steve Adams took shot after shot, trying to kill them as they ran.

Nina's breath caught in her throat. Wyatt could die, and she would be there to watch it happen. *What a nightmare.* When would it stop?

Wyatt caught up to Parker, beside the plane. Nina nearly collapsed, but caught herself. It was time to quit being weak. That wasn't the kind of woman she was, no matter what was happening.

"Let's go."

Nina nodded even as Wyatt took her elbow and ushered her inside. The plane engine roared. He had his phone out already, calling for police even as the plane started away.

Wyatt pulled her toward a pair of seats. "We need to draw Steve Adams's fire away from the ranch. I called the cops. They will keep the Turnels safe."

She tried to think it through. "Do you think he tried to kill Abe because he talked to us?"

"Tying up loose ends. That's what you said, right?"

Nina sucked in a breath and blew it out slowly to regulate her breathing. "You're not a loose end. You're a serious problem." Surprise flashed on his face, so she said, "I just don't think you should sell yourself short. He should be worried, but he isn't going to stop."

Wyatt sat on the seat beside Nina as the plane accelerated. She surveyed him, checking for injuries. He seemed unharmed. Nina touched his shoulders, his neck. His face. He was okay.

Nina's breath hitched. A nice old man who had carried a lot of guilt until that morning had nearly been killed. *Thank You, God, that he was able to tell us all that information.* Steven Adams hadn't silenced him. Abe had been able to say everything he'd wanted to say, to relieve himself of a burden he had carried for years—one that had nearly cost him his life when he'd tried to confront Adams.

There was no way she would let Wyatt end up dead. If Steve Adams was trying to torment her by coming after Wyatt, Nina had to spin that to her advantage. To use it somehow to trap the man so they could catch him.

Wyatt touched her face, and Nina realized she was still touching his. The muscles around his eyes contracted. "I don't want to know what you're thinking, do I? It doesn't look good at all. Maybe you could wait and tell me later."

"Why later?"

"My heart might have calmed down enough by then that I'll be able to handle it."

Nina smiled. "I doubt that's true. You seem to be able to handle anything." And at this point, that was probably a very good thing. Hopefully, even with all this trouble, Wyatt wouldn't decide that enough was enough and let her go. He could choose at any moment to walk away and leave her to deal with Mr. Thomas.

Or worse, stick around to help when she knew it was only because it was the right thing to do. Not because he wanted to, out of care for her.

"That thought seemed like it was even worse." He leaned closer and touched his lips to her forehead. "I'd tell you not to worry, but worrying is probably a solid plan at this point."

Nina couldn't laugh, but her quick exhale said enough.

"I'm right here with you, okay?"

She nodded.

"You're okay. I'm okay. We survived today. Abe Turnel and his family will be safe."

The plane swerved a little but left the ground. Parker yelled, "Seriously? Seat belts, people!"

Nina smiled and they both sat quickly to buckle up. Her brain spun with questions, the foremost of which she spoke aloud. "How did he know where we were?"

"Followed us somehow. Tracked our phones. If he's a former CIA agent he knows enough tricks to keep us in his sights."

"We're supposed to be getting ahead of him. Playing

offense. It was a good idea. Did it turn around and bite us back?"

He didn't answer for a minute. "Abe will hopefully see it differently despite what we risked. If we catch Steve Adams, that is."

"You seem so sure." Nina picked at a thread on the hem of her sweater. "So certain we're going to catch him." She glanced up. "What was it you said outside the courthouse...'I saw your life flash before my eyes'?"

He nodded.

"That happened to me just now." And despite the fact that she thought Wyatt was their best shot at drawing out Steve Adams, that didn't mean she wanted anything to happen to him. If there was a better way, she'd have to think of it. Otherwise they didn't have a whole lot of options left.

"I understand." Wyatt's eyes darkened. "Things are happening neither of us expected. We care about each other..." He waited, so she nodded her agreement. "I knew I liked you, but this is more than that. Do you get what I'm saying?"

"Yes." It was more than just affection for her, too. "But it's not like anything's going to happen."

His brow twitched for a second. "Why not?" He looked confused, hurt even. *Oh, no.*

Nina swallowed. "We're friends, and I love that. But, well. It's just that..."

"Way to let me down gently." He shifted back against his chair.

"Wyatt—" She didn't even know what to say. Why was he surprised? The desire to right the wrong done to her father had consumed her life for years but never produced a result. She'd never had the downtime before now to try and obtain her mom's file even. Now she finally had his real name, and with that came the chance to find him. To bring this merciless killer to justice.

"I just can't think about a relationship right now. I've been all about the hunt for Steve Adams for so long there's nothing else in my life. I already have to get this wrapped up before school starts in a couple of weeks. Then I'll be shaping young college minds, and a relationship will be a completely different thing."

She'd tried to lighten things, but from the look on his face it wasn't working. "Wyatt, I just haven't even considered—" was she really going to have to say it? "—romance. Not once, not really." She was a CIA agent. Who had time for emotional ties, dates, hand-holding and kisses? Before Wyatt, none of those things had ever been a priority.

He was the first man who had ever made her think about any of that. *Why is that, Lord?* Maybe after Steve Adams was brought in they could go for coffee. Have dinner. Explore what was between them.

"Wyatt—"

He put one earbud in, then the other and shut his eyes. "I'm going to try to nap on the way back."

Wyatt didn't pull his earbuds out until they landed. Even then he was quiet on the drive to the office. Yeah, he was shutting her out, but what else was he supposed to do? Here he was growing closer to Nina, seeing her as more than a friend, navigating those fledgling feelings of attraction, and she had straight up said to his face that she hadn't even considered him and romance in the same sentence.

Talk about a slap in the face.

Now he had to regroup. He had seriously thought that something was happening between them. He'd been interested and excited about where it was going. But Nina evidently was still only focused on bringing in Mr. Thomas—too focused, if he had any say in it. The hunt had consumed her to the point she didn't even see what was right in front of her.

Wyatt scanned the underground parking lot as they walked through. Jonah had asked them to check in, probably to reassure himself that they were both fine. There had been a whole lot of near misses the past few days. Wyatt was getting kind of tired of skimming the edge of danger.

If her God was protecting her—and by association, Wyatt—that was all well and good. But what about everyone else? There were some questions that never got answers. He hadn't been a homicide detective without learning that. Some mysteries weren't meant to be solved. But if he was going to put his trust in a God he couldn't see or hear, then Wyatt was going to have to get his answers from somewhere.

Maybe he could sit down with Parker when they had a minute and ask him some questions about why he believed in God. He'd seen the change in his friend, the peace and joy that hadn't been there before. Wyatt knew it wasn't all about Sienna. There had to be something to Parker's having become a Christian or else there wouldn't have been this definite, lasting change in Parker's life that he'd seen unfold.

Back at the office, Nina held back to let him go through the door first. Wyatt swiped his key card and signed her in with the duty marshal. Jonah spotted them and strode across the room with that face that meant he had something to say. Wyatt could use a distraction.

"What's up, boss?"

Jonah lifted his chin. He gave Nina an actual smile, though it was distracted. "Mason Pierce is here."

Wyatt glanced at Nina, who said, "Emily's father."

That was when Wyatt noticed the suited African-American man across the room. Mason Pierce stood in the waiting area outside Jonah's office. His tie had been loosened, and his sleeves rolled up to reveal a tattoo on the inside of his right arm. Wherever he had put his jacket, it wasn't here. Pierce had the look of someone who had traveled all day and was anxious for coffee and a shower, and then bed. Even though it wasn't lunchtime yet.

Wyatt would guess he'd come in the night before on a red-eye flight.

Jonah introduced them, and Mason shook his hand hard enough that Wyatt's hand nearly collapsed in on itself. "Good to meet you." He was far more solicitous with Nina. "Thank you. Both of you. For taking care of Emily and my mother-in-law. I appreciate it."

"Of course." Nina gave him the smile she'd given to Wyatt the day before. The smile that said, *Talking to you is the* only *thing I want to be doing right now.* He'd figured that boded well for the two of them. That she valued his company.

Evidently it was just her being polite.

Still, that wasn't the only thing swirling in his head. "You were deployed, weren't you? You got back pretty fast. It's been less than forty-eight hours."

He didn't back down. Mason Pierce had nothing to hide. "I actually wasn't deployed the last month. I've been in DC. Interviewing with the Secret Service." He shrugged a shoulder. "Gonna need something to do after I retire from the army. I didn't tell Theresa or Emily about it in case it doesn't pan out. They want all this cleared up before they'll move forward." Pierce lifted one eyebrow. "That good enough for you, or do you have more questions before I can go see my daughter?"

Jonah chuckled. "I'll call ahead. We have to check your credentials, get you clearance with the marshals watching them. It'll take time, but we'll get you there before end of day."

Pierce sighed. "Got it."

Nina said, "We can take him over there."

Wyatt had to shake his head. "It's not that simple. Even if we get authorization, Steve Adams followed us to Montana today. There's no way we can go anywhere near Emily."

"But he can't be back already. We left right away. Where was his plane?"

Jonah chimed in. "The cops reported in that Bridget heard no more shots after you boarded the plane, and Abe is a little bruised but otherwise fine."

Nina motioned to Jonah. "See. He wasn't hiding a helicopter or another plane. He'd have to have driven a ways, and then flown back here. He isn't going to know where we're going to be for a while."

"You're talking about a career CIA agent," Wyatt said. "You of all people should know that means he has skills and resources we cannot discount. What if he's tracking both our phones?"

Nina paled.

"We can't assume he hasn't found his way back to Oregon by now. We can't assume anything about this man until we're the ones tracking *him*."

She bit her lip, but nodded. "We need a plan, then."

Wyatt didn't want to put a damper on her desire to see Emily and her father reunited. Nina slumped in a chair while they waited through the procedural aspects of getting Mason Pierce in to see his daughter.

Finally Wyatt got a call. "Yes. Thank you." He hung up. "Mason Pierce!" When he looked up, Wyatt motioned Mason over to his desk. The man had been napping in the same chair he'd been sitting in when they'd arrived, but didn't seem to mind being disturbed. "We're good to go."

He said to Nina, "Emily wants you there, too. She needs to tell you something."

"Okay," Nina said.

Wyatt gave Mason the address, and Mason left first. Nina and Wyatt both left their phones at the office. They also changed clothes, donning what were essentially disguises that would at least throw off Steve Adams. Wyatt extended their drive to the safe house to just over an hour since it was only twenty minutes away. Going around and around in circles had a point sometimes, and today it hopefully helped them lose Steve Adams. If the man had managed to tail them.

Wyatt pulled up around the corner, a prayer on the tip of his tongue. Sometimes the only thing that made the difference between a person being safe and being a victim was the uncontrollable. If there was a God who would keep Emily Pierce safe, Wyatt was willing to ask Him for help.

The marshal outside emerged from the cover of bushes, saw Wyatt and lifted his chin. "Mason is inside."

The marshal in the house showed them to the kitchen,

where Theresa was drying dishes with a towel. She set the mug down and held the towel in her hands, her eyes red like she'd been crying. "Mason is upstairs trying to talk to Emily. The girl hasn't said one word to me all day." She shook her head. "I just don't want to believe she's becoming a teenager. Not yet. Maybe you'll help."

Nina nodded.

Wyatt climbed the stairs after her, not willing to let Nina out of his sight. He hung back in the hall and realized what the noise was. Emily was crying. The preteen looked up from her dad's shoulder and saw Nina. Wyatt saw her face and knew right away that Theresa was correct. Something was not right.

"He was here," Emily said.

"What?" Nina shook her head.

"Mr. Thomas. He was here."

FIFTEEN

Nina crouched in front of Emily while her father wrapped his arm around her shoulder. Their greeting had been warm enough, but clearly there was distance between them. Still, that was something Mason Pierce was going to have to figure out. Though Nina figured it was likely the reason for this move to work permanently stateside. But before their family could master that hurdle, Nina had to bring Steve Adams down.

Otherwise he would torment this girl for the rest of her life.

Emily pressed her lips together. "It was last night. Just after three, because that alarm clock they gave me is so bright it lights up the room, so it was the first thing I saw." She paused. "I don't know what woke me, but he was there. Standing in the corner. Just watching me." She pointed to a dresser, where Nina imagined the man had perched on the surface and waited.

But for what? While Nina had been resting at Wyatt's, unknown, Steve Adams had been here. They'd gone to Montana and come back, and she hadn't said anything. They couldn't assume Mr. Thomas was idle, not when he took every opportunity to move.

Mason shifted. "Did he touch you?"

Emily glanced at her father, a slight frown on her face. "No. He stayed over there. We just talked, and then he walked out the door."

Nina exhaled. This was unreal. She glanced at Wyatt, who stood in the doorway, a door Steve Adams had walked out of. Wyatt nodded. He understood what she was feeling. That the man should never ever have been able to get in this house. *Protective custody.* What were they supposed to do when nowhere was safe for this girl?

Nina turned back to her. "What did you talk about?"

"He told me a story. About a curious little mouse that was free to play all she wanted, but she was hungry for cheese so badly that she got all of her little mouse friends killed." Emily's mouth curled. "It wasn't a very good story. But he seemed to think it was important."

Nina nodded. "It was." She squeezed Emily's hand. "Did he say anything else?"

Emily shrugged. "Not really."

"Nothing about coming back?" Nina saw Mason glance at her as he picked up on the fact her question was significant.

"No. He didn't say that. It was more like he wanted to pass you a message, but I don't really know what it was."

"That's okay, I understand it," Nina told her. "You did great." She was about to get up when Mason spoke.

"Why didn't you tell Gramma or one of the marshals that he was here?" He clearly wanted to downplay his concern, but it was there. A father's heart of love for his daughter even though their relationship had been characterized by the physical distance of his deployment.

"He walked out the door," Emily said. "How could he do that unless one of them let him in and out? I was scared. I thought Mr. Thomas must be friends with one of the marshals or something. How else did he just leave without anyone stopping him?"

Nina explained his history as a CIA agent, and what that meant for his skills at covert operations. He could certainly break into and out of a house without anyone knowing. But he shouldn't have even known where Emily and Theresa were.

Mason turned to Wyatt. "How did this happen?"

Wyatt didn't react, even under the pressure of the soldier's stare. "That is a very good question. One I will find an answer to."

"He could have killed her—" Mason's voice broke. "Hurt her."

Nina still had Emily's hand in hers. She could see the girl grow concerned over her father's reaction, so she squeezed her hand again. "I don't know. We're tougher than we look. Right, Em?"

The girl cracked a smile. Her voice was small, but she lifted her chin. "Right."

"Nothing about this is right," Mason said. "Not one thing."

Nina stood and tugged on Emily's hand. "Why don't you run downstairs and see what your Gramma is doing?"

"I know you just want to talk about me while I'm not here." She stood up. "But whatever. I don't want to talk about Mr. Thomas anyway." Her gaze zeroed in on Nina. "I want to go home."

Nina said, "I'm working on that."

"Whatever." The girl left.

Mason linked his fingers behind his head and squeezed his eyes shut.

"Look, I know how you feel." Wyatt stepped forward.

The soldier shook his head. "You have kids?"

"No."

"Then you can't know how I feel. There's no way."

Wyatt sighed.

Nina took a step closer to Mason, but he cut her off before she could speak. "They're done here. I don't care how 'safe' you deem them. He got in here."

Wyatt's eyes were dark. "We'll definitely be moving them, of course. But we'll also figure out how this happened."

"You had better." Mason paused. To let his words sink in? "Now we finish this. You know what that message was, right? About the 'little mouse.'"

Nina nodded. "That's what Steve Adams called me when I was a little girl. Before he killed my mother." She glanced at Wyatt. "Now we need a plan to draw him out. That's what I'm thinking we need to do. Lay a trap for him, and when he shows up—" She clapped. "Snap it shut." Both men nodded, but neither spoke, so Nina said, "All we need is someone to be bait whom he wants strongly enough to get his attention. Make him come to us."

"No." Wyatt started to say more, but Mason cut him off before he could finish his thought.

"How about you?" Emily's father folded his arms, his hard stare directed at Nina. "So eager to catch him, I'm guessing I'm not good enough bait for that. We can try, and I'd do it just for the chance to get face-to-face with this guy. But I don't see you jumping at the chance to do this. Seems more like you want the marshal here to do it for you."

"Of course I'm going to be the bait," Wyatt said.

She shuddered just hearing the words. "No, you aren't. If anyone is going to be bait, it's me."

"If you're going to argue about it," Mason said, "why don't we make it a party and all go in?"

Wyatt laid his hand on her shoulder. "Nina has been fighting this guy for years. I don't want her near him, though I can understand why you'd want to be part of the takedown of the man who traumatized your daughter."

Mason said, "Seems to me like she's holding up pretty well under the circumstances."

Nina couldn't believe he was brushing it off. Maybe he just needed to feel like things were better than they really were, or convince himself he was making it that way. Or he didn't want to be the bait, and he just didn't want to say that.

But Mason had to wake up, or Emily would be so far gone off the rails he'd never be able to get her back.

Nina said, "He gets in your head. Emily knows that, I know that. He's tied himself to her in the same way he tied himself to me. He thinks he helped us, or that we should be grateful." She swallowed down the hot rush of emotion, determined not to lose control. "This thing consumed my entire life, and now I finally have the chance to end it so that the same doesn't happen to Emily. You think I wouldn't gladly be bait?"

"No." Wyatt squeezed her shoulder. "You're not doing this, Nina. I'm not going to let you."

"Well, then, who is?"

"I am."

Wyatt caught her gaze and motioned with his head for Nina to step to one side with him. They'd spent hours planning. Now it was time to go.

But not before they talked.

Nina frowned, but went with him. She'd barely spoken to him since his declaration that he go in alone. The plan had coalesced to him and Mason, with it being broadcast over the airwaves that Nina and Emily were with them, just to make it all the more tempting for Steve Adams.

Wyatt took her to one of their conference rooms and shut the door. He braced himself for her ire. She hadn't been happy that he was the one to risk himself, while she waited in the van. It was likely this would hurt as much as their conversation in the plane. He was putting himself on the line, along with Mason, to help her fix her problem. She had to realize that.

Wyatt pushed away his twisting thoughts and faced her down. "I just wanted to check in and make sure you're good with the plan."

Nina shrugged. "Why wouldn't I be? Of course you need to be the one to do the takedown."

He didn't miss the sarcasm in her voice, but chose to continue on. "I want you to stick in the van with Parker."

"I'm not going to jeopardize this operation. I have more professional experience than that."

"Look." Wyatt sighed. "I know you wanted to be in on this, but I want you to be safe."

Wyatt had seen over and over agents who had to witness an innocent get hurt just to obey an order. When they couldn't take it and disobeyed the call to hold their positions, things always went wrong. Parker could control Nina, but if she made up her mind and he was distracted for a second, then she could slip away from him and wind up getting hurt.

"Nina—"

"No, I think we're done with this conversation. You

seem to think I can't be a professional, like I've forgotten all my training in the last few weeks." She stuck her hands on her hips. "Just because you're the bait doesn't mean you're the only one in the line of fire. Once we sight him we'll be moving in, and I'll be in the lead. You think you're shutting me out, but you're the one who doesn't see that this is a team effort. It won't be just you out there. It'll be all of us."

Wyatt stepped closer and reached for her.

Nina took a step back. "I don't think so." She shook her head. "You thought I was mad you overruled me. You don't get to make accusations like that and then feel bad just because I pointed out that you're being unreasonable."

"Well, I do feel bad, okay?"

"Doesn't matter. I'm pretty sure you've made your true feelings clear. You're the big man doing the takedown. I'm just the little woman sitting safe in the van."

Seriously? That's what she thought? "Nina, I care about you. I would have thought that was pretty obvious by now. I'm still here. Now tell me why it's bad I want you to be safe?"

"There's no way you could get out of this without us ending him…as a team. But apparently you're not interested in that."

What she said clicked in his brain. "So you do want him dead."

"He wants us dead."

"You know, you might have to face the fact that he's going to be arrested. I won't kill him unless he makes a move to kill me, Mason, or any other officer. It has to be justified, but that's nowhere close to what I'm aiming for. It's not justice if he wants to be dead so he can escape the punishment he's due."

Wyatt took a step back, glad he finally knew what page they were on. "He's controlled your life for so long I don't think you even realize how bad it is at this point. He's sucked you in, made you consider things you'd never even have thought of if the desire to get revenge for what he did to your family wasn't so strong."

"This isn't revenge. It's justice for the team to take him down."

"You think he cares about that? He's got you so twisted around it's like you want to form some kind of club with Emily Pierce. Yes, you both went through something traumatic. But that doesn't make you…what, sisters?"

"I can't care about her?"

"You want to think this is healthy, but it isn't. I think it's gone on so long you don't know how to live without the shadow of Steve Adams in your life. You say you have this great teaching job lined up for your future, but you can't even get in a real relationship." He dropped his hands, realizing he was edging into hurtful territory and ready to shut it down. And he would, in one second. "If you could, things between us would be a whole lot different. But instead I have to shut you out, and you have to stay in the van."

He really, seriously was worried about her. Wyatt wanted good things for her, but it was like she had been damaged by Steve Adams. Maybe a kind of PTSD, he didn't know exactly. But he'd seen it in his father's inability to function when he realized a little girl had died because he hadn't moved faster in the case. True or not, it was how he had processed what happened to him.

Nina was doing the same thing, and she didn't even know it.

Wyatt didn't want to say anything else that would get her upset, so he left.

It was time to go, and as it was he barely made the coordinated meet with Mason Pierce. The whole situation had been orchestrated, and it had to go down right, or they would lose the element of surprise with Steve Adams.

The team element Nina had mentioned wasn't lost on him. That was why Parker and the rest of the guys were there. But Nina would be safe, Wyatt had made sure of that.

She might not want to accept it, but somewhere in all this Wyatt had fallen for her.

Wyatt drove Mason to a house on the edge of town, the place they'd broadcast was the new safe house for Emily and Theresa. Of course it was totally empty. They were taking a lot of chances trying to convince Steve Adams of an elaborate untruth, hoping it would draw him out.

The house was furnished, but with that musty smell of being closed up for too long.

Mason paced the downstairs living area. Wyatt checked his phone, a burner Parker had supplied him with, then clicked his radio. "In position."

Parker answered. "Roger that. Switching to radio silence."

Wyatt didn't want to think about the fact that Nina was in the van, two streets over. They'd set up surveillance, but it was limited to ensure Adams didn't catch onto it.

"Dude, you look like someone kicked your cat."

Wyatt glanced at Mason. Lighthearted in a situation like this? The man was totally military. He knew when to get serious, but he could take the hit of adrenaline and keep on joking. "Sure I don't know what you mean."

"Let me guess. She turned you down?"

Wyatt shook his head.

"Got you all tied up in knots and then shut you down. Seen it before. Dude, it even happened to me. Honestly one of the biggest surprises of my life." Mason blew out a puff of air. "One moment everything's fine, video chats, phone calls. Emails. Then it slows down. Eventually it's a trickle. Then I get divorce papers in the mail. In Afghanistan."

"Harsh."

"You have no idea." Mason shook his head. "Now my kid's a stranger, my wife is the shadow in the room no one wants to talk about and my days are filled with trying to put back together something that's still going to be incomplete when I'm done."

Wyatt nodded, unsure what to say.

"Then I realize I got Emily out of it. Even if I've got nothing but trust issues, an estranged daughter and some good memories mixed in with a whole load of crappy ones—I still have a child. A precious daughter I will twist myself inside and out to win back." Mason went so still it was like he was a statue. He started to talk, made one incomprehensible noise and collapsed.

Wyatt whirled around. The barbs of a Taser imbedded themselves in the vest he wore, but one hit the skin of his neck. The shock of it made his breath catch. The force of the voltage coursed through him, and he blacked out for a second.

He came to when Steve Adams pulled the gun from the holster on Wyatt's hip and shot two rounds into Mason Pierce.

SIXTEEN

The next blast of high voltage bent his body up off the floor. Wyatt could barely think, the pain was so excruciating. When he was finally able to comprehend anything past the agony, he was jostled. Steve Adams's shoulder landed in the center of Wyatt's stomach, air expelled from his lungs in a rush and he realized he was being carried.

How in the world had Steve Adams managed to get past their perimeter? Granted that had been the plan, but it was never supposed to have gone down like this. Wyatt prayed—actually prayed—that Mason Pierce wasn't dead. That Parker had realized the man was shot and was rallying to get him medical attention. Steve Adams hadn't killed Wyatt, though. He was taking him elsewhere.

Not good.

Wyatt couldn't even move his fingers but a twitch. He was essentially incapacitated, though fully aware of what was going on. Really, really not good. *God, I know You're real. I always have, even if I didn't want to admit it. You're Lord of Parker and Sienna's lives. Lord of Nina's life. I want to know more about that before I die. Whether that is in an hour or in fifty years. Keep Nina safe. Don't let Mason die, Emily needs him. And, if You want, could You help me, too?*

Wyatt wasn't above begging for his life. Not when God might be able to preserve it. He'd never thought he'd be the guy who prayed only when he thought he was going to die, but why not? It seemed like a good enough time to him. Especially if it helped.

Wyatt heard a *click*. Steve Adams shifted and dumped Wyatt into the trunk of a car. He couldn't move. He tried to yell, but no noise came from his throat. He reached for his cell phone. Where was it? He couldn't even move.

Street lamps cast a shadow across Adams's face so that Wyatt couldn't read anything in the man standing over him.

Where was the sound of running? Parker should be yelling in his earpiece. Was it still in his ear? Questions swirled in his head. How had Adams done this? How was he getting away with it? Wyatt would die and there would only be more questions left with his demise. Nina would have even more reason to spend her life trying to bring down this killer—her guilt that she'd caused yet another death before she could stop Adams.

They were alike in that way, at least.

Nina.

His heart cried out for her, even as he tried to convince himself she didn't care for him the way that he cared for her. Still, he wanted to see her.

Steve Adams leaned down. "Time to get the girl and wrap this up."

Wyatt strained to see in the dark night, then something sharp pricked the outside of his upper arm. There was nothing he could do. The trap had been a trap of Steve

Adams's own making—taking Wyatt to draw out Nina so that he could get the real prize.

And he had no way to warn her.

After injecting him, Steve Adams threw down the trunk lid and shut Wyatt inside.

The car rumbled to life, and Wyatt descended into blackness.

"What do you mean, something's wrong?" Nina glanced at the surveillance cameras onscreen. "There's nothing on video. No audio."

"Exactly." Parker was already out of his chair. He flung the van door open and jumped out.

Nina shut it behind her and raced after Wyatt's partner. "You think Steve Adams got in already?"

When he didn't answer her, Nina said, "That's not possible. We would have known. Heard it. Seen it. He couldn't have accessed our remote feed and given us false information to make us believe everything was fine. Radio silence was *your* idea. Steve Adams couldn't have known that."

They should have been a team, performing the takedown together. Nina had been satisfied with her part, even while she knew why Wyatt had arranged things like that. And now Steve Adams had destroyed it.

"The target would have accounted for either way." Parker keyed his radio, which put him in contact with the team at large. "Position one to all positions. Check in."

Nina's earbud crackled and one by one they checked in. Except Mason and Wyatt.

"All positions converge. Something's wrong."

Nina heard boots before she saw anyone. Two team members met them in a covered position close to the front door. A faint light in the front window was the only light in the otherwise abandoned house.

"Go."

Parker led the way and they cleared the dining room first. The light she'd seen outside came through from the living room. Which meant someone else would have seen Steve Adams if he'd walked through the area of the house where Wyatt and Mason had been.

"Here!"

Nina followed the call to find Mason on the floor, his hair disheveled and his face flushed and damp. Blood had pooled from a wound on his thigh to stain the wood floor. Parker held a balled-up jacket against the injury.

Nina collapsed to her knee beside the wounded man. "Where's Wyatt?" Parker was already on his phone, calling for an ambulance, but there was no sign of his partner. Didn't he want to know what had happened?

Mason blinked, the lines around his mouth deepening as his face pinched with pain. "Adams shot me and then took him." He shifted and groaned.

Parker said, "Hold still."

Mason nodded and his gaze flickered back to her. "Guess I wasn't the prize."

Nina squeezed his shoulder and looked up as Jonah strode into the room. His boots clipped the wood floor to them. "Steve Adams took Wyatt."

Jonah lifted his hand, a cell phone in it. "We found Wyatt's phone on the grass at the side of the house. We can't track him, but we're on this and he won't get far. Canvassing the streets, knocking on neighbor's doors. Someone will have seen something."

Nina doubted that. The man was apparently able to slip past them, even with surveillance in place. This was supposed to have been a foolproof plan, but instead of getting out ahead of the man they were still playing defense. When was this going to end?

Jonah crouched in front of her. "We will find him."

Nina chewed her lip. She didn't want to say the words. She didn't want to be the one who lost faith right when believing counted the most. But she'd seen Steve Adams's work before. If he was determined to end Wyatt, there was nothing she or any of them would be able to do to stop it.

She took Wyatt's phone from Jonah and stood. An ambulance pulled up outside, but she ignored the EMTs, walking onto the sidewalk and down the street. She should call Wyatt's cousin, the FBI agent. Parker probably knew what the pass code to Wyatt's phone was, and his cousin might be able to help them locate where Steve Adams had taken him.

She spun back to the house. Parker was inside, and she could see him pace back and forth in the dining room. He looked like he was yelling into his phone. He probably knew about Wyatt's cousin. They probably had a system in place for precisely if something like this happened. A plan that didn't include her, and didn't require her help.

Parker looked up, out the window. He saw her and shook his head as he shrugged like, *what are you doing out there?* Nina turned back to the street. She sat on the hood of a car parked at the curb and pulled out her own phone.

Wyatt had been gone for who knew how long. Probably up to half an hour, if not more. What was he thinking? Was he even still alive?

Was it her fault?

If she'd been the bait, then maybe Steve Adams would

have taken her and left Wyatt…or shot him like he'd shot Mason. And wasn't that the reason Wyatt had assigned her to the van? But what if this, too, was part of Steve's plan?

Nina choked down the emotion and pulled up her contact list and found the number Steve Adams had been contacting her from. She opened a new message and typed, Where is he?

She tapped the phone on her leg and waited. She hoped he was busy and that she could distract Adams somehow, maybe even long enough to find the two of them before Wyatt was killed.

Even while she wished it were she who'd been taken, Nina was glad she was the one who got to put all her skills toward finding Wyatt.

If anyone could, it was her.

Bile rose in her throat. She hung her head to suck in big gasps of breath. He was going to die before she could tell him that she loved him. He'd gotten completely the wrong idea about what was happening between them. Not to mention seriously misinterpreting her, assuming she thought a certain way without even asking her.

So things were complicated enough that they didn't need to jump into anything. But did he let her explain that? No.

It was a wonder she didn't want to kick dirt in his face, or whatever women did these days when men angered them. But if he was alive, if she could keep him from being killed, Nina likely was going to do the complete opposite. If she saw him again, she'd likely kiss that dumb confused look off his face and then explain a few things.

Romance wasn't even in a spy's vocabulary. Then she'd been searching for Mr. Thomas. Excuse her for not seeing what had been right in front of her face until it was too late.

She really hoped it wasn't too late.

Nina loosened her death grip on the phone and dialed the number instead. First, before she could find Wyatt, there was a serious list of things she needed to say to Steve Adams. That sadistic killer was going to get a piece of her mind.

A muffled sound came through the phone.

Nina was ready to lay into the man, no matter that it might make him angrier. "Where is he? I want to know." She paced. "And you better not have harmed one tiny hair on his head or you'll have me to answer to." She didn't care that she sounded ridiculous. Not when Wyatt's life was at stake.

"N-Nina?" His voice was raspy and quiet. She could barely hear him. It sounded like he was in a closed-in space, confined somewhere with no way out.

"Wyatt? Where are you? Are you okay?" She sucked in a breath, trying to tamp down the cold fear that had settled in her stomach. She had to let him talk. With Wyatt's phone, she brought up the little menu that let her turn on the camera light for a flashlight without needing to unlock the phone. While he collected himself, she shone it through the window at Parker.

Please let this get his attention.

"I think. I don't know where I am." He slurred the words, sounding disoriented. Steve Adams must have given him something to force his compliance, or he'd injured Wyatt.

Parker winced and glared at her. Nina pointed to the phone and mouthed, *Wyatt*. "Are you hurt?"

"No."

Parker raced out the front door in time to hear her say, "Any idea where you are?"

Wyatt's partner got on his phone again, yelling about traces and GPS. Nina stepped away and pressed her finger over her other ear so she could focus on him. The man she loved. Maybe since she'd first met him, she didn't know. It was possible, since she'd never felt like this about anyone before.

"I'm in a box." He shifted around, and the pitch of his voice rose. "Nina. I think I'm in a coffin."

Parker started to yell louder. He had to be able to hear the conversation now.

"There's a tank in here. Like an oxygen tank."

Nina's heart plummeted.

"One second." After Nina had counted from five he was back. "It's a timer."

Nina spun. Her eyes locked with Parker's, and—she was sure—the same dread on his face reflected on hers.

"Nina, I'm running out of air." A beep signaled something on his end. There was a rustle and he said, "Low battery." He paused for a split second. "Bye…goodbye, Nina."

"Wyatt!"

It was too late. The phone cut off.

Nina fumbled with the phone, trying to redial. "Wyatt!" She had to speak to him. "Wyatt!" What else was she supposed to do? "Wyatt!" He was alone…in a box…running out of air.

Parker grabbed the phone.

"We traced the call and got a location. The team is moving now. Get a hold of yourself. If I have to stand here and make sure you don't pass out, that operation is going to take longer. And that's time Wyatt does not have."

"You were listening."

He grabbed her hand and pulled her along. She glanced back to see Jonah sprinting after them. Nina needed to suck it up and get it together, otherwise she was going to fall apart completely. Parker drove them in his SUV to the place they'd traced the phone call's origin to.

Nina sat in the back. It wasn't like Steve Adams to be so sloppy he would lead them right to where Wyatt was being held.

Jonah hung up his phone. "Paxton's team was closest. They're headed inside already."

Parker nodded, his fingers tight on the steering wheel.

Seemed like they thought this was good, but something in Nina just wouldn't settle. And it was more than simple concern for Wyatt's life.

Parker raced through the streets until they pulled up outside a two-story office building for lease. "He's probably inside there somewhere."

Jonah nodded. "Basement or some kind of closet. A boiler room, that kind of thing."

Both men cracked their doors and climbed out.

Nina reached for the handle when her phone beeped. She looked at the screen. *Baltimore Public Library.* She opened the message, eager to hear something from Wyatt. He had to be okay enough to send a message, and to have decided it was worth the battery usage.

Boom.

Nina blinked at the screen. She glanced up. Parker and Jonah, guns drawn, jogged toward the building. Why would Wyatt… Nina opened the door, stood on the step and yelled over the door, "Park—"

The building exploded.

A wave of sound and burning-hot air rushed toward her. Nina was flung backward onto the road, where she landed on the concrete and rolled.

The phone screen flashed, the only sound in her ears the rush of air as though miles away. Nina lifted the phone with her dirty, scratched-up hand.

Drive.

Nina wanted to throw up. Drive? She found the keypad, dialed 911 and put the phone to her ear. Nothing. She checked it. Dialed again, coughing against the smoke and ash. It wasn't working. What was wrong with her phone?

Dread settled over her.

Steve Adams.

Nina rolled to try and see Parker or Jonah. With the smoke and flames she couldn't make out much. She could hear sirens in the distance, though probably closer than she could hear. Parker and Jonah were probably deaf, given how close they had been. *God, please let them be okay.* They hadn't been right up close to the building, but feet away. *Please, God.*

The phone vibrated this time. How was Steve Adams controlling her phone? And how was he messaging her from a phone that Wyatt had? She dismissed immediately the idea that Wyatt was involved. It was far more likely that Steve Adams had the technology. That he'd cloned that phone.

Get in the car and drive.

Nina rounded the car. Her body hurt, but it was nothing compared to the men who had been inside that building. Were they okay?

Nina turned the SUV on. Did Steve Adams know Parker had left the keys in the ignition?

Parker got up, mouthed something she couldn't hear. Red and blue flashing lights rounded the corner. Nina checked the backup camera and hit the gas.

When she'd turned the corner the phone vibrated in her lap. At the next stoplight she looked down and checked it. The maps app was open on her phone as though she had searched for a location herself. Steve Adams had hacked her phone. He knew exactly where she was, and he was directing her to the center of town.

When she arrived at the destination, Nina pulled to a stop, not willing to put the car in Park and allow the vehicle to unlock the doors. She didn't want anyone getting in.

The car went dark. The engine shut off. All the lights. Everything, as though someone had flicked a switch and turned the whole thing off. Nina lifted her foot off the brake. She pressed the gas. Tried to turn the key. What was happen—

Her door opened and all she saw was an arm. And then sparks.

Everything went black.

SEVENTEEN

Nina regained consciousness in a room. She shifted on a bed and took the place in. Motel, if she had to guess. Her head was a fog, her body bruised like she'd been hauled and dragged with no care for whether she was being injured.

She rolled and tried to sit up, but found her hands were caught. Handcuffed. To the metal rail of the headboard.

Her head whipped around. Was he here? Had Steve Adams brought her here for who-knew-what horrible purpose she didn't even want to think about?

She sucked in a breath and yelled, "Wyatt!"

Even if he wasn't here, maybe she'd draw attention from a neighbor and someone would come help her. There was no reply. An exterior door to her right was locked. No one could get in. If she could get free of the handcuffs she'd be out the door in less than four seconds. The other end of the room was a door, likely the bathroom. Was Wyatt in there?

Nina's best friend had been found after a particularly nasty operation facedown in a bathtub, unconscious. That wasn't something Nina wanted to relive. Especially not if this was going to wind up like some crime show on TV where there was nothing left but mess and evidence.

God, I don't want to die. We were so close. It's slipping out of my fingers, and I'll lose him completely if I die. If Wyatt is gone. Her breath hitched. *Don't let him be gone, Lord. I can't handle another death because I didn't find Mr. Thomas fast enough. If he's dead I might as well give up now and die, too.*

What was the point in living if the one man in years that Nina had come to care for, the one man she'd thought she might actually love, was gone? Aside from a job she'd accepted just for the sake of something to do, and a best friend who was now living her own life, Nina had basically nothing.

Nothing but a lifelong obsession with finding the man who had destroyed her family. And now she was at the end of the journey facing the fact that he was about to destroy her, too. That years of searching, hoping and praying she might be able to do this were all wasted effort, pointless frustration that now might turn out to have been useless.

The bathroom door opened, and he emerged. Same clothes he'd been wearing before, minus the jacket. He'd rolled his sleeves up, and his hair was perfect as usual. His shoes were even shined.

"Nina." Her name was a breath on his lips.

She clenched her stomach, trying not to freak out. "I know you're Steve Adams. I know everything about you, everything you've done."

He stepped closer, unfazed by her words, grasped the chair at the desk and flipped it around. He sat, crossed his legs and clasped his hands together. "You will address me as Mr. Thomas."

The distance between them didn't make Nina feel much better. Not since she was trapped with nowhere to go and no way out. *God help me.*

"These past few days have been…unpleasant. But I feel that we can put that behind us and move on, don't you?"

Nina was silent as she tried to figure out what on earth he was talking about. Move on to what? And *unpleasant*? He'd purposely led them to his real identity and now he didn't want to acknowledge that's who he really was.

When he said nothing else, Nina said, "What do you want from me?"

"My patience has been tested, Nina, but no more. This is your last and final chance to cease these ridiculous attempts to best me and finally surrender. Admit that you cannot have the victory."

He looked so…normal. It was as though he was commenting on a day of uneventful weather. "Now is the time for you to finally be free, Little Mouse. Your life has come to a close, and you will forever be freed from this world. I had thought you would be grateful for the freedom I've given you, but it seems you are not satisfied. Therefore, despite the fact that I have given you everything you should have wanted, my Little Mouse must be silenced. Forever."

"You killed my mother, and you think you did me a *favor*?" Nina screamed. "It wasn't freedom. You condemned me to a lifetime of grief. You gave me nothing! You only took from me!"

His mask slipped a tiny bit, and she saw a flash of anger in his eyes. "You will be free."

"I will not. You destroyed my life."

He launched out of the chair. "I made you! You were

nothing until I came along." His voice was a roar in the otherwise quiet room.

Why hadn't someone heard her yell? Why wasn't someone helping her? "Where is Wyatt? What did you do to him?" Nina shifted on the bed, trying to get away from him, but her back hit the headboard. "Is he dead? Did you kill him, too?"

"This is your last chance, Nina. You will be free as this Wyatt is."

Wyatt was dead? "You may as well kill me. I have nothing left."

"What about your delightful friend, Sienna? It would be such a shame if she met a sudden demise. Especially when she is with child."

Nina writhed against the bite of the handcuffs. "You don't touch her! I'll kill you!"

He leaned forward. A couple more inches and she would be able to make contact. "I find that unlikely."

"I will. You know I will."

"Do I? None of the others put up the fight you have, getting their friends to shoot me. Some of them even thanked me for making their lives better…at least up until that end. But I gave their daughters what they needed." He looked aside. "The freedom to do what they wanted to do instead of mother controlling every second of her life. Ballet. Violin. Painting. Until her feet were raw and her hands bled."

He looked at Nina then. "I set her free."

"And now it's my turn?"

He nodded. "Now you will cease this bother and be free. Forever."

"I'm not going anywhere, and you no longer consume my life. Because I've given my heart, all of it, to Wyatt.

There's no more room for hatred for you. That's all there ever was. And now you're nothing. Not anymore."

Steve Adams launched himself at her. Nina kicked out before he could hit her and caught his cheek with the heel of her boot. He cried out, reached behind him and pulled out something a little bigger than a handgun.

He touched it to her neck and she quit moving.

Nina blinked again and woke. This time inside a wholly different kind of room. It smelled like earth after rain, and already her clothes had begun to stick to her body because the temperature was so warm. She shifted and heard the *clink* of handcuffs. So she was still wearing them.

Her hip felt like one giant bruise, and she figured Steve Adams had thrown her in here. Wherever "here" was. She couldn't see much, since the only light was a yellow street lamp peeking through a couple of high vents.

On a long exhale, Nina sat up and tried to shake off the feel his words had left with her. Even if she died in here, it couldn't be worse than facing down him and his sick desire to kill her. Like he was doing her a favor and not just still tying up loose ends. Trying to get away with murder.

Nina looked around. This was his end?

It looked like a shipping container, but there was nowhere in their Oregon town where there would be one. How far from home was she now?

Nina kept turning, shuffling around without getting up. One leg was numb from the pain in her hip, and she didn't think she had the strength to stand just yet.

Behind her, she saw a long box and gasped. It looked like…a coffin. Or at least a box similar to ones that would transport a body. In the center of the container, it was the only thing in there with her.

Wyatt?

It was circled with some kind of thick tape, and she could see wood between the strips. She scanned the floor with her gaze and felt around with her fingers until she snagged something sharp. It looked like a shard of glass. She started at the end closest to her, under the lip, and began to saw at the tape.

"Wyatt?" She called his name, and the sound echoed through the metal container. "Wyatt, are you in there?" She kept sawing, cutting through the tape even though the glass sliced at her fingers. What if she got it open and he was already dead? Was she prepared to face that outcome?

Nina didn't know if she could handle it. What she did know was that she'd spoken to him, and he'd been running out of air. If she was the difference between him living and dying then it didn't matter that her fingers were getting slick with blood. That the glass was slipping, that she was messing this up.

She'd been messing it up from the beginning because she'd been too scared to realize how she felt about him. She'd hidden behind the professionalism that had defined her career, and missed all the signs that he cared for her. And that she cared for him.

What was that about? Nina of all people knew how short life was, how easily it could turn and leave a person reeling like being tossed around in a storm. Wyatt had steadied her. Faith had given her that strong foundation, the rock that could not be moved, but Wyatt had held her hand through it. He had been a gift of companionship and peace from God, one that she didn't deserve.

And she'd taken him for granted.

Hot tears tracked down her face. She brushed them away with the back of her hand, leaving grit and probably blood smears instead. Who cared? He was probably dead anyway.

Nina sank back on her heels and sobbed.

A rustle from within the box...the *coffin*.

Nina moaned aloud and fell backward with nothing to break her fall. Whoever was inside shuffled. The top burst open from the corner she'd sawed. His fist emerged, disappeared and then came out again. Over and over he punched away the wood until it splintered.

He coughed. Nina cried louder as he sat up.

He looked at her, breathing heavy but looking relieved. And very much alive.

"Wyatt."

Wyatt took a breath of musty air and tried to relax his heart rate. Adrenaline rushed through him; pricking beads of sweat gathered on his forehead. He glanced at Nina and soaked up the sight of her. She was beautiful even with mussed hair, wide-eyed and looking like she was so happy to see him.

The smear on her face drew his attention. He glanced down at her hands, stained a dark color. Wyatt hauled his heavy body through the hole he'd made in what he now realized really was a coffin. He could barely process what had happened.

He'd seriously been trapped in a *coffin*.

So Steve Adams intended him to be dead, then? And evidently Nina also, given that she was here with him.

Wyatt's legs didn't quite cooperate, and he collapsed onto the floor. "Where is he?"

She blinked. "I don't know. I woke up alone, and I was until you came out of there."

"Thank you for that." He shifted closer to her. "I wouldn't have gotten out if you hadn't broken the tape." He held out his hands. "Show me."

She hesitated, but lifted her hands and placed them in his. Wyatt swallowed down the nausea and unbuttoned his shirt so he was only in his jeans and his undershirt. He wrapped his button-down around her hands. "It's not clean, but it's the best I can do right now. Hold it tight so it helps slow the bleeding."

She nodded, and he reached for his pockets, emptying everything he carried on the floor. Everything he usually carried, except for his cell phone, his weapon and the backup he wore in an ankle holster.

He rummaged through his wallet, but found what he was looking for. Wyatt used the handcuff key to release her. Nina exhaled. "Now we just have to get out of this container."

She nodded, but there was no hope in her eyes. There was only a quiet despair. She thought Steve Adams had won.

"Nina, we're both here. We're together, and we're going to figure out how to get out of here. He isn't going to win. I don't care what he said or did, he isn't the one in control here."

Her brow flickered.

"While I was in there—" he pointed at the coffin he didn't really want to dwell on too much "—I was thinking. And I prayed. God brought you here so I could get out. So I could then help you get out. It was Him, not Steve Adams." He touched the cheek that wasn't smeared with his hand. "Who is in control?"

Her voice was quiet, but she said, "God."

"Not that madman. Okay?"

She nodded.

"I thought I was buried alive. I thought I would run out of air." He sucked in a breath trying to tamp down the remnants of the fear he'd felt coursing through him as surely as she felt it now. "But I wasn't, and now I get to be with you."

He leaned closer to her face and rested his head alongside hers so he could just feel her there with him and breathe. Life was so precious, but if she wasn't here with him then it was barely worth living.

How had she come to mean this much to him in so short a time? Wyatt could hardly believe it. And while she might not exactly feel the way he felt, he figured he could show her enough how valuable she was to him. How much he loved her. Maybe eventually she would trust his feelings for her enough to begin to love him back.

God, I know I'm asking for a lot today. But maybe You could help me out. She's here with me for a reason. Maybe this is it?

"What if we can't get out? What if no one finds us?"

Wyatt stroked her cheek with his thumb. "You're going to lose faith in me now?"

Nina's lips curled up into a small smile. One that disappeared almost as fast as it came. "It's hard."

"I know. But I thought I was going to die, and you got me out. Now you only need to trust me, okay?"

Nina bit her lip, but nodded.

"Good." Wyatt went back to the coffin and reached around. He didn't need the oxygen tank, but he shut it off. No sense in wasting it if he might need it later. His fingers made contact with the phone, and he pulled it out.

"Maybe there's enough juice in this thing we can call for help. Maybe there will be enough signal we can send a message. That's a lot of maybes."

Nina smiled at his ridiculous attempt at lightening the situation. He was so enamored with that smile he leaned in and gave her a quick kiss on the lips. She blinked, but he was already leaning back. Wyatt got up and paced the length of the container, looking for a possible way out. He liked that he had surprised her, the fact that he had that element of surprise on his side. If he could keep her off balance long enough to charm her, she would see that he was someone she should keep around her. That he could make her life better the way she was making his better.

Okay, so not right at this moment, since they were stuck in a container. But more generally, she had shown him his worth in a relationship that he'd never seen before. She'd let him be himself, to show her his flaws and still embrace him even though she knew the worst of it.

Wyatt pulled on the handle and tried to push the door open. Nothing. It didn't even budge one inch. He went to the vents and tried to haul himself up high enough to see out, but all he could catch a glimpse of was a cloudy night sky and street lamps.

He turned the phone on. There was a little battery, but it was blinking low and about to run out altogether. If they were going to use it, they'd have to do it quickly.

He waited a minute, but no bars popped up. He turned back to Nina. "Nothing. No signal. We have no way to call for help."

EIGHTEEN

Hope sparked inside Nina despite the pain now reverberating through her hands. "They can trace the phone, can't they? If it's on, then they can track it." She told him about the signal they'd traced to the warehouse that had exploded.

"If Parker's okay, he'll be running down any lead trying to find us." But he didn't say what she was thinking...that to find them, Parker needed to be able to track their phone's proximity to the closest cell tower. Which required a signal.

"I stole his truck."

Wyatt smiled like it was no big deal. Maybe even funny.

"I left him and Jonah, and they could be really hurt."

"You said you saw Parker after the blast. I'm trusting that they're fine."

Nina looked away. "He wanted me to go with him. He said he was going to hurt Sienna and the baby." She shuddered. He'd been so close to her. So determined that she go with him. Until she'd told him that she belonged to Wyatt.

Now Steve Adams had dumped her in here with him. Were they supposed to just sit here until they died of starvation? She glanced around. They were trapped, but for what purpose? It didn't seem like that effective a way to dispatch them if he really wanted them dead. Unless Steve Adams would rather they suffered for days before they died. That seemed likely.

Wyatt came over, the phone in his hand. Their only way to contact the outside world, but he'd turned it off. *God, we need a signal to call for help.* Or did He want them to get out on their own? Maybe they were supposed to figure this out like a riddle. But the cuts on her hands were bleeding, and she didn't think Wyatt was as fine as he was pretending. There was a sluggishness to his movement, a carefulness to every step that said he wasn't convinced he might not collapse at any moment.

They had to get out of there.

"I have no idea where we are. All there is outside are yellow floodlights. I can't get high enough to see the ground, and even if I could I doubt it would help." He sighed. "We can't get out of here without someone opening the thing from the outside."

"And no one knows where we are."

Wyatt settled onto the floor beside her. "We're okay for now, right?" When Nina shrugged, he said, "So we wait a little while, keep checking for a phone signal. Next time I turn it on I'm going to hold it up by the vent, see if I can get something from up there."

"He probably has some kind of signal blocker in place. Maybe we'll never be able to call for help." *We'll die here.* She didn't say it out loud, but the words still hung in the air between them. Nina was losing faith. She was losing hope. It was too hard not to think that Steve Adams had won.

Nina glanced up at the vent as though she might see

him lurking there to watch their suffering. As though Steve Adams had put them in here like some kind of twisted science experiment so that he could watch the life drain from her.

"I thought he was turning himself in to us. I thought he wanted to be caught, that he was done. But it was still just a game." She took a quick breath. A gasp. All she could do as she fought the overwhelming surge of emotion that threatened to break her. "It was always about getting to me, and we managed to best him a couple of times. To ruin his plans. But he still won. He was one step ahead of us even at the end, and now it's gotten us nowhere. We're going to die in here just like he wanted, and it's for nothing."

Nina couldn't think straight. Tears tracked down her face.

"I know it's hard, Nina. But you have to let all this out."

"He'll know he's won."

"He isn't here."

Nina shook her head against his shoulder. "He always knows. I've never done anything he didn't know about. He's been watching me, following me for years. I know it. Even when he was away, killing those other women, he always came back and found me. I know it."

"Things are different now." Wyatt leaned back so he could take her puffy, damp face in his hands. "He hasn't won. We're not dead, are we? We're just in a jam."

Nina shook her head.

"Don't argue with me. I'm right. I know I am. This is a sticky situation, and it doesn't look like there are many options to get out of here. But we have time to figure it out, don't we? He isn't here. There's no immediate threat to our lives. Right?"

"I can't believe you're pretending this is fine. We're going to die in here." She knew she was basically shouting in his face, but she couldn't help it. He was crazy if he thought they were fine. This was the end and she knew it. There was no way out. They were out of gas at a dead end with a hurricane coming that would sweep them away. Only Wyatt was pretending not to see it.

She shook her head. "He's going to get away with all of these murders and it'll be because we weren't good enough to stop him. Who knows how many more he'll kill? I'll have to answer for their deaths as well. I won't ever be able to escape him, not even in death. And I'll have to accept it."

She swallowed. "Maybe that's what God wants. Maybe it was prideful to think I could bring Steve Adams down. All these years chasing him, believing I could do it, believing I had right on my side. Maybe I was kidding myself. Maybe God thought I needed to learn to be humble, and that things don't always go my way."

"Not at the expense of people's lives."

"I know that, but they're still on my conscience." She paused. "But what if I'm not supposed to bring him in? What if I'm only supposed to lay down my desire to see him get justice? It might not be the path I have set before me. It might be someone else's job to bring him in because I'm too close to it."

Wyatt studied her face.

"Maybe I thought too much of my own ability to get the evidence. To finish this. What if it wasn't what God asked from me?"

"Would He do that?" Wyatt said. "Would God ask

you to do something like that, to watch your life's aim be taken away and given to someone else?"

Nina shrugged. "What if He wants to know that I'm going to trust Him even if that is the outcome? Maybe that's the point and I've just missed it all along. God teaches us every day, but we miss it because we're not listening. What if I've spent *years* missing it because I wasn't listening?"

Wyatt's jaw worked back and forth. "Are you listening now?"

He knew next to nothing about faith or being a Christian, but he wanted to learn. Nina was showing him something big, something hard for her to grasp even though she'd been a Christian for years. As painful as it was for her, he was excited. One day he would have the kind of relationship with God where he would hear the Father's voice like that. To know what He wanted instead of seeing him as he did now—as a benevolent Creator, but not yet a Father.

Nina nodded. "Yes. I'm listening now." She smiled. "I guess you could say He's gotten my attention."

"Maybe that is the point of all this. I certainly am."

Nina's brow crinkled. "I'm listening." She glanced around the container. When she got up, Wyatt moved back and watched her do a circuit of the container. Was she praying? He could see how she'd need a little peace to be able to talk to the Lord for a minute about all the concerns she had. Nina had had a very long, very difficult week. And while it hadn't been peachy for him either, she was emotionally exhausted and close to breaking entirely. Only her faith—and hopefully his being there—were allowing her to hold on.

He was trusting God now. Parker and Sienna had trusted God when they were in danger, and Nina's relationship was such a benefit to her he could see it. Why not do the same? He needed to learn more about how it worked for sure, but if God really was God, then Wyatt could trust a being that powerful to be stronger than Steve Adams's plans.

"Here."

"Huh?" Wyatt glanced at her.

Nina stood on tiptoes and peered up at the corner of the container. Wyatt went to stand beside her. He reached up to where she pointed with her hand still wrapped in his shirt, which was now stained with blood. She wouldn't last much longer with the blood loss without going into shock. He needed to keep an eye on that.

His finger hit something smooth, plastic maybe. He tugged at it and it came out, attached with a wire. A hole had been drilled in the corner, at the highest point, and this had been poked through. Wyatt pulled on it until the thing dangled down. "A camera."

"He can see us."

Wyatt pointed to where it hung against the wall. "He can see the floor now."

"Do you think he can hear what we're saying?"

He shook his head. "It's not that type of camera. Video only—I wouldn't guess he has audio. Just enough to see that his plan has come to fruition."

"What plan? Freaking us out to death?"

Wyatt didn't exactly know what was going on in the container either. What purpose was there in locking them in this place and watching? He had to be close by, with a camera like that. Or using some kind of internet connection. Wyatt paced down the container and back.

What was Steve Adams waiting for?

It wasn't a foolproof plan if he couldn't be certain they wouldn't get out or be rescued before they died.

Wyatt looked at the coffin, then at the door. He strode over and grabbed the air tank. It wasn't full, so lacked the weight he probably needed, but he didn't care. He was done waiting around for someone to find them, or for Adams to kill them.

He lifted the tank and brought it down on the handle as hard as he could. The vibration of the metal nearly made him drop it, the sound deafening. He looked back to see Nina trying as best she could to cover her ears.

He hit it again and again, bending the metal, but it wasn't enough. No matter how many times he hit the door handle, it didn't budge. He threw the air tank aside and pushed against the door. With all his strength, Wyatt cried out as he tried to open the door.

His body sagged and he sank to the floor.

Pulled out the phone.

Whispering a prayer, Wyatt turned it on.

A grinding sound, like metal on metal, begun outside the container. The noise grew from quiet to a loud noise that filled the whole place.

Wyatt raced to the vent, but couldn't see out. He handed Nina the phone and dragged the coffin to the window. He stood on the top as carefully as possible and peered out. A crane circled toward them. There was a loud *clang* of metal on metal again, and then an engine revved.

He could see the ground, but it wasn't dirt or concrete. The whole area was nothing but mounds of gravel. Different kinds of stones, rocks. A quarry? Someplace that sold chippings for driveways, or to landscapers? He racked his brain to try to think where in town that was. It was a long shot that the place he was thinking was actually where they were. But how did it help?

It was the middle of the night, the early hours. Someone was here to operate the crane, but he didn't think it was likely an employee. A security guard might be around. But if Steve Adams was here, watching them, intending to kill them somehow, the security guard was likely dead.

Nina gasped. "There's a signal!"

Wyatt raced to her and caught up the phone. The intermittent signal was back. Praying hard, he punched in Parker's number. The phone beeped low battery, and he had to dismiss that indicator with a click of Okay. It felt like an eternity before his partner answered. "Please be Wyatt."

"Alvarez gravel."

"Thank you, Lord." The phone beeped again. Parker's voice cut out for a second. "...our way. Hold tight."

The phone died.

"Yes!" Wyatt nearly jumped up and down. "They know where we are. They're coming." He lifted Nina, careful of her hands, and kissed her thoroughly. "We're getting out of here."

"I hope so. I hope they get here in time."

The crane started up again. There was a *clink* like the links of a chain. The sound moved all the way above them like a line that ran up a tower all snapping tight. The container shifted. He lost his grip on Nina as the floor moved and they began to sway.

She slid down the floor. Wyatt followed and they slammed into the back wall. The container swayed. "Wyatt!"

He couldn't grab her hand or he'd hurt her. If he held her they would bump into each other. Instead Wyatt moved farther away and climbed over the coffin so the wood was between them. The container swung as though suspended in midair.

"Where are we going?"

"I don't know." It was all Wyatt could say. He didn't know what Adams was doing, but one thing was certain.

"We're going to die now, aren't we?"

Wyatt nodded. "I'm going to pray you're wrong."

He'd hoped Parker would get there in time, but his partner might not. Wyatt and Nina could die right there, trapped in the container while help raced toward them.

Not fast enough.

Not strong enough.

Not good enough.

There wasn't much in his life that Wyatt was proud of, given the way he'd ignored his father for so long. The way he hadn't admitted to Nina how he felt about her.

The crane shifted and they started to descend. Down into a hole? The bottom of the container hit something and the walls creaked and groaned as they settled, not flat but off-kilter.

A machine whirred above them. Gravel and sand began to pour into the vents. Not enough to suffocate them until they ran out of air, but the container was being buried.

With a groan, the container began to lean. Wyatt made his way back to Nina. He couldn't let the two of them die before he told her how he really felt about her.

Wyatt gathered her into his arms. She held hers around him, gripping him with her forearms, but not touching him with her injured hands. He stared down into her eyes. "You're the strongest person I know, and it's been a privilege to help you out the past week. But that's not all that's happened." He took a breath. "I've fallen in love with you, Nina."

She smiled. "Me, too, Wyatt. I'm so totally in—"

The whirring stopped and the room went totally black.

They were buried.

NINETEEN

All Nina could hear was the rush of her own breath in her ears. Her legs threatened to buckle under her and send her crashing to the metal floor, but Wyatt's arms held her up.

"Should we try to find that air tank?"

"It was almost empty when I broke out of the coffin. It won't be much use now." Wyatt gave her a comforting squeeze, and she tried to make it enough.

They leaned together against the back wall, as the container had tipped with the force of sandy dirt hitting them. The opening was now above them and to the right, taunting. It could be above the surface, but it was locked. If it weren't locked, they still weren't strong enough to push it up and open so that they could get free of this metal box.

They would be buried there forever, and no one would ever know that a container had been buried under the dirt.

Sienna and Parker would never know what had happened to them. Their lives would go on, but without Wyatt and Nina to share in the joy of their baby's birth. Seeing his or her first steps, or first day of school. Nina sobbed, the sound echoing in the container.

Wyatt's arms tightened. "Hang on, okay?"

"For what? Death?" Her laughter sounded harsh even to her own ears. "That's all that's going to happen to us. He won. I don't know why I didn't realize all along that I was fighting a losing battle. I should have realized."

"So you're going to lose faith now, when it really counts?" His voice was flat. He had to be worried; Nina didn't believe he wasn't. That would have been impossible. Maybe he needed the reassurance, though. Maybe he needed to see that her faith held steady, even now. But was it able to withstand this? Nina wasn't sure she even knew.

She squeezed him with her arms and settled closer as she began to pray out loud that Steve Adams's plan would somehow be thwarted. That their phone call to Parker would mean the difference between life and death. She prayed for the faith to believe, even when she couldn't see a way out. And wasn't that what she had needed her whole life?

Faith had kept her from going insane when life threatened to bring her to her knees. Nina hadn't buckled yet. Was she going to allow Steve Adams to make her do it now?

She began to end the prayer, and Wyatt started to speak. His words were tentative, as if it wasn't quite natural yet for him to speak to his Heavenly Father. Nina's eyes filled with hot tears as she listened to his simple prayer that they would somehow get out of there alive.

Nina set her head on his chest and let the tears fall. Wyatt said, "Amen," and she echoed it through the sobs. She'd never have thought they would end up here, sharing a prayer, thinking they were going to die. She wouldn't even have imagined it was possible; she'd tried so hard to focus on catching Mr. Thomas that she hadn't left any room for romance.

And now here it was.

Despite her plans, despite her intentions. Nina had gained so much in Wyatt, and yet she hadn't achieved the thing she'd thought she needed so badly.

Catching Steve Adams.

It was a long shot that Parker would find them before they suffocated, even after the nearly-empty oxygen tank ran out. It was a long shot that—even if he did get here in time—Steve Adams wasn't still here and waiting. His surveillance had to be down, but he might be hanging around until he was sure they were gone. Parker might be walking into a trap.

"He'll come," Wyatt said. "I know he'll come."

How he had so much faith in his partner, Nina didn't know. Wyatt did kind of sound like he was trying to convince himself. She didn't blame him. After all, what hope did they have left except what they'd expended in that prayer?

And yet it didn't feel as if it had been exhausted. It almost felt like, through saying that prayer, it had strengthened the little faith Nina had. Maybe even given her more.

Nina smiled at him in the dark, even though he wouldn't be able to see her. "I didn't get to say it earlier. But I think, even though I didn't want to need you, I do. I didn't want to need anyone. I thought I could do this by myself. But I'm really glad that you're here, Wyatt. Because I've fallen in love with you." Nina took a second to bask in the fact that was completely true. "And if I'm going to die here, there's no one I'd rather spend my last few minutes with."

The air was getting thin. It was getting harder to pull

in enough air to talk. Eventually they'd have to sit. They would get sleepy. Nina didn't want to suffocate, buried alive. "I'm glad you're here with me so I don't have to be alone."

"I'm glad about that, too." He squeezed her again and then pulled her down so that they sat side by side on the hard floor with her still in his arms. "The worst thing about waking up in that box was being alone and not knowing what was going to happen."

The muffled sound of machinery starting up broke the silence once again. Nina cut off what she'd been about to say. "What was that?"

She felt Wyatt shake his head. "I don't know."

A steady thump, like rain on the roof, began. Something was coming down on top of them. Nina stiffened. "He's burying us. He wasn't done. Steve Adams is still here, and he's covering the container so no one will ever find us!"

Wyatt's arms loosened. He shifted and they both listened to what was happening above them. It sounded like dirt coming down on the roof and pouring across the top to the lowest corners, where they were sitting directly underneath.

The feeling of being trapped, present since she'd woken up, came back to swallow Nina. She tried to suck in more air, but the oxygen was hot and made her feel like she was going to burn up.

Wyatt tugged on her arm. "Calm down, Nina. You're having a panic attack. Breathe, just breathe, or you're going to pass out and leave me alone in here to face this by myself."

His words cut through the sheer terror in her mind so that what he said penetrated. Nina found the will to fight this drowning feeling. But would it be enough? She didn't want to die feeling nothing but fear.

Metal scraped against the container. Nina cried out. "What is he doing?"

"I don't know." Wyatt's words sounded far away.

The machinery cut off and someone was yelling. Nina couldn't make out the words, but it sounded like more than one person. Did Steve Adams have help?

The door clanged and then creaked. Nina slapped her hands over her ears to shut out some of the noise. It was unbearably loud, so loud it felt like her ears were going to split open. And then it was over.

"Wyatt?"

Nina glanced up. Flashlight beams shone in their faces. Nina shielded her eyes and Wyatt said, "Parker?"

"You guys okay?"

Nina didn't even know what the answer to that question was. She didn't think she would ever be okay again, not after what had happened. Was it really over? "Where is Steve Adams? He might be there. You might be in danger. Everyone needs to watch out!"

Parker said, "We are, Nina. It's okay. We're going to get you out."

"He might be out there." Did she want to come out if it wasn't safe? She didn't want to stay in this death box, but what choice was there? He could blow their heads off.

"We're okay." Wyatt's touch was as reassuring as his voice. "He can't get to us. We'll be protected."

"Parker needs to find him." Nina couldn't do it anymore. She was giving up the fight. She had to, or she wouldn't be able to stay sane.

"Okay." Wyatt nodded. "Parker will find him, and I'll help."

She wanted to tell him to stay with her and be safe, but that would be selfish. He needed to help his partner, and a man like him wouldn't allow another to take the risk when it could be shared.

Steve Adams didn't have a chance.

Wyatt grasped Parker's hand and let him haul him out of the basket he'd been lifted from the container in. The fresh night air filled his lungs, so much better than the air he'd been choking on. Parker was covered in dirt, his clothes and arms and hands. As though he'd tried to dig them out himself.

Wyatt grabbed his partner and hugged him tight.

Parker slapped his back so hard Wyatt winced. "Love you, too, brother."

Wyatt laughed. "You wish. I'm just glad to be alive, and your ugly face is the first thing I saw. Don't take it personally."

Parker laughed as well as what they left unsaid floated between them. Neither of them believed for one second what Wyatt had said was the truth, but it wasn't like he was actually going to say, "I love you" out loud. Nina, yeah. Parker…no way. They'd been partners for long enough now that Wyatt would miss the former SEAL. That was enough.

"Where's Nina?"

Parker motioned to the side with his head. Wyatt turned and saw Nina and Sienna in an embrace like the one he'd just shared with Parker, only without the manly slapping. Wyatt smiled. Sienna caught it and mouthed, *Thank you.* He nodded to her and then turned back to his partner. "So where's Steve Adams?"

Parker frowned. "He was long gone when we got here.

We found a security guard passed out, but we're hoping when the EMTs get him to come around he'll at least be able to give us something. We've also got someone going over the footage. It's motion activated, so when he used the crane we're hoping it was caught on camera."

"I'll be praying for a car make and model and license plate, not a shot of Adams playing construction worker."

Parker lifted his chin. "Oh yeah? You'll be *praying*."

"Don't look so smug, okay? I catch on eventually."

Parker slapped him on the shoulder. "Good for you." He gave Wyatt a gentle shove toward Sienna and Nina. "Let's talk."

They reached the women, and Nina frowned. But she was looking at Parker. Wyatt glanced at his friend and said, "What is it? What happened?"

Parker gave a short nod. "Mason Pierce is in the hospital. Last word was he'll have some recovery to do, but he'll be okay long-term."

"That's good, at least." Wyatt didn't think that was the end of it.

"What about Jonah?" Nina said.

"He's okay. We were only banged up, no permanent damage." He paused and studied Nina's face. "I'm guessing Adams texted you—that's why you stole my truck and left Jonah and me on the sidewalk?"

Nina nodded.

"She was trying to save me," Wyatt said.

"I'm not saying it was the wrong thing to do, not when it led us to the two of you. Although I'm not sure why Nina felt the need to put herself in harm's way in the process. But we were fine. It just wasn't the smart thing to do."

"It worked out, didn't it?" Parker shot him a look.

Wyatt put his arm around Nina both to comfort her and to show his partner that he needed to back off. Nina didn't need any more grief today. All of them had been through so much.

"Fair enough. We can unpack the whole thing later." Parker sighed. "So Adams decided you've been enough hassle he was going to get the two of you out of his way. But now what? You know him best, Nina. Where would he have gone?"

Nina glanced aside. They were silent while she thought about it. Eventually, she said, "I don't know. Emily and Theresa are safe, right? I can't think of anyone else. He's probably long gone, moving on with his life. What he wanted to do here is done. I didn't think there was anything else when he thinks we're dead." She looked at Parker. "You're sure Theresa and Emily are okay?"

Sienna pulled out her phone. "I'll call and make sure." She stepped away.

Nina didn't say anything while Sienna made the call.

"Okay. Thank you." Sienna looked up, her face dark. "You were right, Nina."

She froze under Wyatt's arm. "He took her."

"Jonah tried to contact the marshals on her protection detail, but no one is answering their phones. He's going over there now himself, and he's sending police units, too. He's going to call back as soon as he finds out why no one is answering."

Nina pulled out of his grip. "No, no, no. This is my fault."

Wyatt turned her so she could see his eyes. "You don't know what has happened, and whatever it is isn't your fault. He thinks you and I are dead. Emily found the picture of Steve Adams—maybe he feels she needs silencing, too. But we aren't going to let that happen."

Her gaze darted around. They were surrounded by people, but Nina was deep inside her own head, where Steve Adams's reign of terror continued. "He's got her, I know it. She's just a kid." Nina sucked in a breath, looking green enough she might be sick. "She's just a kid."

Wyatt gathered her up in his arms. "You don't know yet that anything's happened. It could be a technical glitch that's put them out of contact."

"You seriously believe that?" She screamed the words at him.

Wyatt winced.

"She's as good as dead, just like we were. You don't know what he's like, what he said to me in that motel, Wyatt. She's twelve. He's going to *destroy* her."

Wyatt set his hands on her shoulders. "I thought I was going to die, but I didn't. I know we prayed, and Parker found us. That's what I know. This is scarier than you can imagine, Nina, but you have to breathe. If he took her, then we'll find him."

"We will," Parker said. "You think we won't hunt him to the ends of the earth to get that girl back? We would do that just for what he did to you, Nina. What do you think we'll do if he really does have Emily?"

Nina sucked in a breath, but she nodded. She had to. They were practically willing her to accept what they were saying, leaving her no choice but to agree. Wyatt loved her even more for her compassion for the girl, even though it was fear right now. Nina felt so deeply he could hardly stand to see the light of it, blazing from her.

Sienna's phone rang. Nina gasped and spun to her friend, but Wyatt kept his hold on her. He leaned down and spoke in her ear. "Even if she's gone, if Steve Adams took her, we're going to find her. We won't let him touch her. We won't let him hurt her. Okay? I need you to believe we'll do everything possible."

"But it's like your father's case," she moaned. "The one we couldn't save."

"And I'm exactly like my father." Wyatt felt the release of admitting it out loud. "I knew I would be as cut up as he was if that had been my case. But Emily isn't that little girl who was killed. She's still alive, and we're not going to let her be Steve Adams's last victim. He's done, Nina. I'm telling you right now. He's done."

TWENTY

They strode as a group to the office, a portable building that didn't look like much on the outside. The place where Steve Adams had tried to bury them alive had turned out to be a gravel pit. Nina couldn't stop shaking. Emily had been taken by Steve Adams.

She tried to think—if she'd known that in the motel, would she have made a different choice? *The motel.* Why did Nina want to think about that some more?

But the thought of having gone with him, and maybe trying to escape later, only made her sick. He'd never have let her go, and no one would have ever found her. Wyatt might have died. As selfish as it was, Nina needed to believe this was the best option because at least now they could pull all their collective experience together and have the best and fastest hope of finding Emily before Steve Adams hurt her.

Emily had been through enough, and this would only add to the trauma. They had to get to her before he did any kind of permanent damage, the kind from which she would never recover.

The office was a bank of computers on desks littered with papers. A uniformed employee sat running his hands through his hair and muttering under his breath. The goose egg on his forehead probably didn't feel too good.

The motel.

Nina sat at a computer by herself and pulled up an internet search engine. The others were scanning surveillance footage for sight of…

She turned to them. "Wait. He didn't disable the feed?"

The employee nodded gingerly. "Actually he tried. We've had so much of a problem with vandalism that our security company set up a kind of backup system. Your guy cut the main feed, but missed the secondary signal. To shut that down you literally have to destroy every single camera. Cost a mint, but saved us thousands in repair costs and repainting over spray-paint tags."

Nina frowned.

The man added, "It's my brother's company."

Nina glanced back at her search engine. She had no idea which motel Steve Adams had taken her to. While they scanned the surveillance video, she shut her eyes and tried to remember what she'd seen and heard. Anything she could dredge up might help them find Emily, or where Steve Adams might have taken her. Because without some kind of clue, they had nothing. No idea.

Nina sucked in a breath and blew it out slowly.

Traffic. The sound of cars driving past, high speeds. Some even overhead.

Nina pulled up a map of the freeway and found a spot where it arced over a seedier part of town. Low-budget motel, cash only. There was a line of four motels in a row, but only one was under the overhead freeway, actually an on-ramp.

The question was whether that was the place he'd taken Emily, to try to do that scene over. To get himself a different outcome to his plan, the outcome that he wanted. Nina tapped a pen on the top of the desk.

"Bingo!" Parker's yell jolted her from her thoughts. She spun in the chair just as he pointed to the screen. "Silver Buick. I'll call the plate in, get an Amber Alert out."

He strode from the room, not wasting a minute of Emily's time. Nina watched him go and saw Wyatt's attention was on her. He frowned. "What did you find?"

Nina motioned to the computer screen where the map was still up. "I think I know which motel he took me to."

Sienna said, "You think that's where he took Emily?"

"I have no idea, but I guess it's possible. He might think I couldn't identify it, that the location is safe." She shrugged. "It's all I could think of that might be helpful. At least until we get something back off the Amber Alert."

Wyatt's gaze roamed over her face. He nodded. "Okay, let's go."

Before she could answer, he hauled her from the chair and out the door. Sienna followed to one of the SUVs, a smirk on her face. But Nina didn't have time to ask her what that was about before he opened the door and practically lifted her into the seat. "Let's go!"

She saw the fear in his eyes, fear that they would be too late. It was the same fear she was feeling. Sienna got in the back, and Parker joined them. Wyatt took the keys from Parker and tore out of the parking lot. Nina grabbed the handle at the top of the door and held on as he tore through town.

Sienna leaned forward and put her hand on Nina's shoulder. Nina set her free hand on Sienna's, grateful for the support of her friend. She'd been alone so many times on missions it was strange to have people here with her, supporting her in this time of crisis, but not unwanted. In fact, she was soaking up this feeling of togetherness. Of family.

Sienna whispered, "I told you so."

Nina shook her head, but didn't let go of her hand. Yeah, so Sienna had been right about Wyatt and Nina. She didn't have to gloat.

Steve Adams had tried to take it away from her and Wyatt, but they'd overcome his plans. Now they were going to make sure he didn't take Emily's future from her.

Wyatt parked outside the office. They hung back while he got in the motel manager's face, showing him a picture of Steve Adams and demanding to know when he checked in. Nina didn't know what time it had been, or what room. But the manager produced a key.

Nina put it in the key-card lock and hung back. Parker entered first, gun drawn, followed by Wyatt. Sienna was in the car, because no one wanted her anywhere near Steve Adams when she was pregnant.

"Clear!"

Wyatt came back out, and she saw it written on his face. "It's empty. She's not here."

Nina nodded, but the tears came hot and fast. She crumpled against the building, not caring who saw her lose her cool so thoroughly. They all felt the same way. They all cared what happened to Emily. They all knew what being acquainted with Steve Adams had cost her over the years.

Sienna came over, but didn't crouch and offer Nina comfort. When Nina looked up, she saw why. "Mason Pierce left the hospital. He slipped out from under marshal guard, even with the crutches. Somehow he got a change of clothes and a car. He's gone." Sienna paused and frowned. "They're looking for the car. But if he can find Emily somehow, why stop him?"

Parker hugged his wife to him. Sienna continued, "And the Amber Alert? A gas station attendant called in. He spotted Adams a couple of minutes ago when he stopped to refill."

Wyatt hauled Nina to her feet, and they raced to the car again. Sienna got the address, and they pulled up at the gas station minutes later. Parker was on the phone with police dispatch. Nina glanced back to see him cover the phone with his hand and say to Wyatt, "Keep going along this street. Take Portrait to Halvern."

"Got it." Wyatt swung the wheel hard to the side, the SUV's lights and sirens clearing a path for them to race through.

"They have him cornered on Halvern where it dead-ends."

Nina covered her mouth with her hand. It wasn't above Steve Adams to use someone as a human shield. But when they pulled up behind the barricade of cars, there was only Steve Adams, standing with his hands in the air as he faced off against a crowd of police officers.

She climbed out, but it was Wyatt and Parker who raced to stand with the officers. Adams's rage was clear as he glared at both her and Wyatt. They had bested him, and now he knew it.

"Where's Emily?" Parker's command was clear. "You've got nowhere to go. This is the end of the line, Steve. Now do the right thing and give us Emily."

Steve glanced to Parker, the glare still in place.

"Where is she?" Wyatt yelled. "Where is Emily?"

Steve Adams shifted, his arms lowered.

"Don't do it!"

"Hands up!"

Nina frowned at the scene. What did they think Steve was going to do?

She watched as the man lowered his arms and reached with one hand behind his back. Wyatt and Parker yelled, but he locked his eyes with her and brought around a gun. Before he could fire, the police did. Nina covered her ears to shut out the deafening boom of each shot. Steve Adams's body jerked several times, and he fell to the ground.

The moment the gunfire stopped Wyatt ran to the car. Where was Emily? He called her name over and over, but heard nothing. He pulled the backseat door open. Nothing. She wasn't there. Parker strained to open the trunk with his fingertips while Wyatt pulled the keys from the ignition.

Nina stepped up beside him as he turned the key and pulled it open, a prayer on his breath. If she wasn't here they would never find her. If she was dead, if Steve Adams had killed her, Wyatt didn't know how he would survive it. He would make the same turn as his father had. He would retreat from everything and everyone—including Nina. Their shot at a relationship would be over before it had barely begun.

Emily Pierce looked up, tape over her mouth, and her hands and feet tied. She whimpered, and Wyatt gathered her up. "It's okay now. Everything is okay."

Worried he was squeezing her too hard, Wyatt loosened his grip. Relief washed through him. He needed to call his father and tell him that it hadn't been condemnation that caused him to pull away from him. No, in fact it was that they were so much the same. Wyatt would never have been able to handle losing a child either. But because of God's grace he had found new life, and Emily had been saved.

Wyatt didn't know why one girl had died and this one had lived. All he knew was that overwhelming sense of gratitude flooding his heart.

"Thank you, Lord."

Parker clapped him on the shoulder and then shut the trunk. Wyatt set Emily on it so Parker could cut the tape on her hands and feet. Nina reached for the tape on her mouth. "This will hurt." A determined look flashed in Emily's eyes. "Okay, girl," Nina said. She pulled at the tape in increments and managed to get it off.

"Are you okay?" Wyatt almost didn't want to ask, but if she wasn't they needed to get her to a hospital. "Did he hurt you?"

"No. He just threw me in here."

"Em!" Mason Pierce wobbled over to them on crutches.

"Daddy!" The girl hopped off the trunk and ran to her father, who caught her up in a hug.

Wyatt exhaled for what felt like the first time in days. Nina chuckled and he gathered her to his side, pulling her close enough they could get a good hug in. She laughed more. "Don't smell me. I think I need a shower."

Wyatt smiled, but didn't let her go. "I know I need one."

"Yeah, you both stink."

Wyatt looked at his partner. He kicked out with his leg, but Parker dodged him. "Nina and I are leaving."

"You should be going to the hospital."

"I'm fine," Nina said.

Wyatt rubbed his hand up and down her back. "I'm fine, too."

It was finally over. They were finally free of Steve Adams. Nina was finally free of him. Emily was being treated by EMTs, and with time the emotional trauma would heal. Her father was home, and he would recover from his wounds.

Parker and Sienna were both unharmed, and Sienna was having his baby. Wyatt had found peace with his father, and though they still needed to talk and get back to the relationship they once had, things were at least on the mend.

"It's over."

Wyatt pulled back and looked down at her face. "I'm thinking more that things have just begun."

Nina's smile eclipsed her face.

Wyatt leaned down and kissed her.

EPILOGUE

Eight months later

Wyatt had been right. Things had only just begun.

Nina touched her fingers to the glass as she stared at the tiny person Sienna and Parker had made. For hours Nina had waited in the hall for word everything was okay, that little Melody had been born and that mom and baby were healthy. Now Auntie Nina couldn't stop staring at the little creation.

The corners of her mouth curled as Nina looked at those tiny lips. That tiny nose. She couldn't think of a time in her life when she had been happier. Things with Wyatt had been going well, their initial long, sweet phone calls and dates developing into spending more time together. Nina was enjoying her teaching job. Wyatt was hinting that he'd like to buy a bigger place, that it was time.

Things were perfect. In fact, they were almost too perfect.

Wyatt had never once mentioned the fact that Nina had—repeatedly—pushed him away in those early days, when they'd been battling Steve Adams. All that was almost a distant memory now, but the concern lingered. Nina hadn't wanted to bring it up, not if it was going to rock their already precarious boat. She'd done better since they started dating, embracing what her life was now and trusting the Lord to guide her through it.

And why couldn't she dismiss the worry? Why couldn't Nina be happy now that she basically had everything she'd ever wanted?

The echo of Sienna's voice counseling her to put aside the anxiety and just live, to be happy, made her smile more even as it frustrated her at the same time.

Why couldn't she just be happy?

"She's pretty cute. Though that's probably because she looks more like Sienna."

Nina turned, the smile still on her face. Wyatt was covered in sweat, dirt smeared across his face and the ball cap he had on. He still wore his bulletproof vest, was still armed and the star badge of the marshals was clipped to the front of his vest. "Did it go okay?"

"I'd rather have been here."

Nina shook her head. "It was boring, waiting hours to hear." She leaned closer to him. "Although hearing Parker shout at everyone was pretty funny. That man does not deal well with his wife being in any kind of discomfort."

Wyatt cracked a smile that made him look a little less exhausted.

"But everyone is fine now. Melody is here, and Sienna is sleeping."

He turned to stand shoulder to shoulder with her at the window. "She is seriously adorable."

Nina nodded. She couldn't agree more, though guys backed off when they thought a woman was baby crazy. Everyone knew that. It didn't stop her from wanting one of her own someday. Or even four. There was a lady at church who had nine kids, and she made it look so easy.

"I want one." Nina slapped a hand over her mouth. She'd said that aloud!

"I'm thinking we should have two, because one would be outnumbered by us and with three there's always one left out. With two, they always have someone to play—and fight—with."

Nina pushed off the window and took her time lifting her gaze to his face. He'd thought about having a family. He'd said *us.* Was he serious? Her heart leapt with hope. "Us?"

"Maybe it's too early, but come on, Nina. It's been months." He stepped closer, looking more like he was chastising her than happy. "You're it for me. I've known it since I met you. It works, you and me. Once you get past the fear you'll realize it, too."

"I'm not afraid."

Wyatt had the audacity to smile. At her. "You're more afraid of your own emotions than you ever were of Steve Adams."

Before she could respond, he swept her up in his arms and kissed her. Nina squirmed, because he smelled as bad as he looked. "You need a shower." Her voice betrayed her humor.

Wyatt apparently didn't think it was funny, because he wasn't even smiling. "You love me."

"Yes, I do. And you love me."

"Why did it take us this long to say that for real?"

Nina tipped her head to the side. "Maybe because we're each as stubborn as the other."

He smiled then. "That's probably true."

"Set me down."

"Are you going to let go, and be happy?"

"Can I tell you that I'll try?" Her life had been a crazy mess of danger and fear, and she wondered if she'd ever fully let go of it.

"I'll accept that." He sighed, then got down on one knee and held out a tiny blue velvet box with a ring in it. One perfect diamond glinted at her.

Nina froze. "What are you—"

"I've had this with me for weeks, waiting for the right time. I guess this is it." Wyatt's eyes were full of hope and a tiny bit of fear. Was he worried she might say no?

He smiled, and it wobbled. "Nina, will you—"

She launched herself at him. "Yes!"

Wyatt stood with her in his arms and kissed her again. "—marry me?"

Nina grinned at him, and Wyatt burst out laughing.

* * * * *

If you enjoyed DEAD END, look for these other great books from author Lisa Phillips, available now.

DOUBLE AGENT
STAR WITNESS
MANHUNT
EASY PREY
SUDDEN RECALL

Dear Reader,

Thank you so much for joining me for my sixth Love Inspired Suspense book! It encourages me greatly to spin an exciting tale interwoven with the truth that God desires to speak into our hearts: He is faithful, and He loves us.

Nina and Wyatt had a tough road to walk together, and a fierce enemy to face. The same is true of us and the giants we face in our own lives. But God's heart is to hold us up through it, and to use those experiences to shape us into the people He has called us to be.

I hope I have many more Love Inspired Suspense books to come, and that you'll join me for each of them. Until then, God bless you richly.

If you'd like to email me, my address is lisaphillipsbks @gmail.com. You can also join the mailing list on my website, www.authorlisaphillips.com. I also love to receive letters from readers, and you can write to me c/o Love Inspired Books, 195 Broadway, 24th floor, New York, NY 10007.

In the strong name of Jesus,

Lisa Phillips

SPECIAL EXCERPT FROM

Love Inspired
SUSPENSE

*Desert Valley's new police chief must hunt down the
woman terrorizing his town and keep her from hurting
the dog trainer he's coming to care for.*

*Read on for an excerpt from
SEARCH AND RESCUE,
the exciting conclusion to the series
ROOKIE K-9 UNIT.*

"I'm going to make a quick run to town and back," Sophie
told newly minted police chief Ryder Hayes and noted his
scowl in response.

"Be careful. You may have been a cop once," Ryder
said, "but you're a dog trainer now."

That was a low blow. Sophie clenched her jaw.

"We all have to be on guard," he said. "There's no
telling where Carrie is or whether she's through killing
people."

"I agree with you. I'll keep my eyes open," Sophie
said.

He arched a brow. "Are you carrying?"

"Of course." She patted a flat holster clipped inside the
waist of her jeans. "I won't be out and about for long. I'm
going to the train station to pick up a dog."

"Why didn't you say so in the first place?"

She was still smiling a few minutes later when she
parked at the small railroad station and climbed out of
her official K-9 SUV.

A sparse crowd was beginning to disembark as she approached. She shaded her eyes. *There!* A slim young police cadet had stepped down and turned, tugging on a leash. "Hello! I've been expecting you. I'm Sophie Williams."

"This is Phoenix," the young man said, indicating the silver, black and white Australian shepherd cowering at his feet. "I hope you have better success with him than we did."

She grasped the end of the leash, gave it slack and took several steps back. She politely bade him goodbye, turned and walked away with Phoenix at her side.

"Heel," Sophie ordered.

The dog refused to budge.

She faced him. "What is it, boy? What's scaring you?"

A loud bang echoed a fraction of a second later. Sophie recognized a rifle shot and instinctively ducked.

The dog surged toward her. She opened her arms to accept him just as a second shot was fired. Together they scrambled for safety behind her SUV.

Don't miss
SEARCH AND RESCUE *by Valerie Hansen,*
available wherever
Love Inspired® Suspense *books and ebooks are sold.*

www.LoveInspired.com